MW01231979

WHAT SHE DESERVES

DELANEY DIAMOND

Garden Avenue Press

What She Deserves by Delaney Diamond

Copyright © June 2021, Delaney Diamond

Garden Avenue Press

Atlanta, Georgia

ISBN: 978-1-946302-47-2 (Ebook edition)

ISBN: 978-1-946302-49-6 (Paperback edition)

Cover photography: Ashley Byrd at lifestylevisualz.squarespace.com

Cover model: @tiffanysharonda on Instagram

This book is a work of fiction. All names, characters, locations, and incidents are products of the author's imagination, or have been used fictitiously. Any resemblance to actual persons living or dead, locales, or events is entirely coincidental. No part of this e-book may be reproduced or shared by any electronic or mechanical means, including but not limited to printing, file sharing, and e-mail, without prior written permission from Delaney Diamond.

www.delaneydiamond.com

Rashad strolled through the venue, sipping champagne with his date, Natasha, on his arm. As co-owner of a financial services firm, he was representing the company at a silent auction to raise money for the Girls & Boys Club, an organization close to his heart.

"I would kill to get that," Natasha said, eyeing the painting on the far wall with a spotlight highlighting the canvas.

The framed watercolor was a field of poppies, with a stormy sky in the background.

"Where would you put it?" Rashad asked.

"In the sitting room at the front of the house, where everyone could see it as they entered."

He could absolutely see her doing that too. Natasha liked to show off, and having a famous artist's work visible as guests entered her house was exactly what he could envision her doing.

She stifled a yawn. "You still up for a late-night meal before we go back to my place?" she asked.

"I am, but are you? That was a pretty big yawn."

She giggled. "Don't worry about me. I can stay up."

Natasha was a sexy woman. Tall and slender with large, gamine-like eyes and a great mouth whose kisses promised a night of wild sex. She was an attorney, working for one of the biggest law firms in the city and had a huge case load that sometimes meant long days, so he was sympathetic to her plight if she didn't have the energy to continue the date after they left. That didn't mean he wasn't disappointed. This was their second outing, and with the evening going so well, he'd hoped to spend the night at her place and wind those long braids around his fist as he hit it from the back. But because of her yawn, he doubted she had anything left to offer but sleep. And he'd had no intention of sleeping.

"I can stay up too," Rashad quipped.

She laughed and slapped his arm.

He chuckled, but the laughter died on his lips when he saw outside through one of the windows. Rain poured down in heavy sheets from the night sky.

Natasha followed his gaze. "Oh boy, it's really coming down out there. Glad we're in the parking garage and don't have to make a run for it, though maybe that's not such a bad thing. Rain can be so cleansing."

Another reason to like her, she was down to earth. She wasn't fussy about her appearance, and instead of worrying about her hair, she would have been willing to run into the storm.

"I wouldn't let you do any such thing. I'd get the car while you stayed behind, nice and dry."

"Oooh." She did a little wiggle. "My hero."

Rashad laughed. Maybe he *was* getting laid tonight.

They continued their leisurely stroll, checking out the available items. He looked at the weekend getaway for two at a luxury resort, which he'd bid on earlier, but two other people had written a higher bid. The trip would be the perfect gift for his assistant for Administrative Professional's Day, so he added his bidding number below theirs and offered significantly more.

"How much longer do you want to stay here?" he asked.

"Not too much. Matter of fact, I'm ready to go if you are, but

I need to dash to the bathroom, and then we can leave. Meet you at the exit?"

"Works for me." Rashad watched her walk away, her braids swinging from side to side in sync with her confident strides in a simple black dress. He smiled a little to himself as two men turned to watch her pass by.

Walking toward the exit, he wound his way through the well-dressed people in the room. As he sidled past a small group of four, the woman in the group caught his eye. He couldn't see her face, but the back of her body and the way her shiny black hair spilled past her shoulders gave him pause. A loose-fitting dress in powder-blue flowed over her curves to her ankles and exposed her shoulders with its spaghetti straps.

Then she turned her head to the left, laughing as she gently tapped the arm of the man beside her, and he saw her profile. That's when his heart ceased to function. The whole world moved in slow motion, and sound receded into the background. He stared in disbelief as she turned her head again so he couldn't see her face.

Rashad stood there for a moment, frozen as his mind played details of their relationship like a quickly moving slide show. Having her squeeze his arm while hiding her face in his shoulder as they rode the Ferris wheel. A weekend trip to Myrtle Beach where they splashed in the ocean and made love by candlelight each night. Her curled up on the sofa in his hoodie and sweats as they watched TV. The gut-tearing pain of their breakup and the silence in his condo long after she was gone.

"Layla?"

He said her name softly. Too softly. She didn't hear him over the buzz of conversation in the room.

Drawn to her, he moved closer and tried again, this time louder and in his normal voice. "Layla."

Her head swung around and so did the head of the man she was with. Her eyes went wide, and her lips parted. She was so damn beautiful that beautiful wasn't enough of a descriptor to truly express the entirety of her appeal. Gorgeous was a more appropriate word, and she was all woman—with lush breasts, round hips, and a fantastic ass.

Rashad remained in place, struck by her unmatched beauty and the way she was always so well put together. Layla didn't do running in the rain. She wouldn't want her hair wet or her makeup to run.

Maroon lipstick covered perfectly formed lips that looked moist and were deliciously soft. Fake lashes brought attention to her soul-deep brown eyes and gave them a seductive, take-me-to-bed look even when she simply looked surprised, like right now. At the sight of him, color temporarily marred her tawny-gold complexion and reminded him of their passionate nights together—his relentless need to claim her body, his burning desire to hear her hoarsely cry out his name and rake his back with white-tipped nails as she spasmed around him.

Rashad swallowed past the lump in his throat, fighting the urge to crush her to him and find out if her lips were as soft as he remembered.

"Hi. What a surprise." Her eyes darted to the Black man beside her, whom he immediately recognized as Ethan Connor. Layla rested her fingers on his arm. "Would you excuse me for a minute?"

Her touch appeared intimate to Rashad and cut through him like a knife. Were they together now?

"Sure, take your time," Ethan said, returning to the conversation. He looked like money in a tailored suit, and Rashad was pretty sure that was a platinum Patek Philippe on his wrist.

He followed Layla to a corner of the room, so many questions burning inside his head, he had a hard time figuring out which to ask first. "What are you doing in Atlanta? You visiting?"

"I... ah, no..." She suddenly looked very uncomfortable.

"Are you... are you back?" He could barely get the words out, barely acknowledge the excitement that immediately spiked in his blood.

"You could say that." Her face shifted from unease into cool stoicism.

"For how long?" He needed every single detail she could give him.

"For good."

"How long have you been back?" he asked, shocked.

"For a long a time. Look, I don't think—"

"For how long?" He had to know how long they'd lived in the same city without him having a clue.

She tucked her hair behind her left ear, a nervous habit that meant she was uneasy. "I never moved to D.C."

Her answer floored him. She'd said she was moving back to D.C. after they broke up because her family was there and she needed a change.

"You lied to me?"

His question had been asked a little too loud and prompted two people to turn and look at them.

"I didn't lie, I... I intended to move when I told you I would, but I never did."

Rashad swallowed the tightness in his throat. "You never said a word. You let me believe..." A flare of anger forced his mouth closed.

"We were broken up, Rashad, remember?"

"Yeah, I remember."

"Then what difference would it have made if you'd found out that I was still here?" she hissed.

"It would have made a difference. I would have reached out to you. I would have..." What the hell was he saying?

He stuffed his hands in his pockets and stared out at the rain. He was stuck in this terrible limbo state of wanting to learn more while knowing he had no business, no right to learn more.

"What are you doing here, right now?" he asked.

"Ethan invited me. He didn't want to come alone, so I came with him."

She angled her head higher and tossed a look of defiance at Rashad, as if daring him to comment.

"Are you seeing him? Just now, the way you touched him..."

"That again?" Her eyes flashed angrily.

Ethan Connor was her boss. Layla was his personal assistant, available to him during the day and sometimes at night. By all accounts, she made a pretty nice salary, but Rashad had always been uneasy about their relationship, and that had caused problems between them on more than one occasion. The guy was worth billions, and at times Rashad wondered if he wanted more than assistance from Layla.

"Forget I asked," he said.

Layla laughed sourly, crossing her arms over her chest, which only served to highlight the lushness of her breasts that peeked above the V-shaped neckline.

"I can't forget, because you're doing the same nonsense you did before. I answered all your questions before about Ethan, and that wasn't enough."

"You liked to make it seem as if I was overreacting where he's concerned, but how do you think it made me feel knowing another man was taking care of my woman?"

"He's not another man. He's literally my boss."

"Who pays for your loft."

"It's a perk of my employment, and I didn't keep it from you. The topic didn't come up, and when it did, look at how you reacted." Ethan's company owned the building she lived in, and he gave her the loft free of charge to use.

"Forget I said anything, all right? It was a reflex." He'd always acted like a jealous fool where Layla was concerned, but he needed to calm down and gather more information.

She glared at him.

"Are you going home after you leave here?" Rashad asked.

"You mean, instead of going home with Ethan?" Layla asked.

"No," he replied slowly. "I mean, are you going home, or do

you have other plans? With your girls or anything?" *Or with another man?* his brain silently asked.

"Yes, I'm going home after I leave here." Her arms fell away to her sides. "Look, Rashad, I'm working. I know you think being a personal assistant and showing up for events isn't real work—"

"That's not true. I know you work hard—"

"But, I am working and don't want to talk to you anymore. Good night."

✢ 2 ✣

Rashad grabbed her wrist before she could walk away. His fingers tightened in a near-plea to stop, wait. He needed to hold on to her a moment longer.

He edged closer. "Can I call you?"

Layla backed up, something flaring in her eyes as she tipped her head back to look up at him. "I don't think that's a good idea. We broke up for a reason."

He forced out one of his disarming smiles to tear down the barrier she had erected between them with her cold voice and even colder eyes. "I just want to be friends."

Anyone listening to their conversation would not possibly believe that, but he had to try.

A faint smile crossed her lips, but there was no humor there. Only silent mockery and a sort of... disappointment.

"You haven't changed, have you? Still the smooth talker. Still working your charm on the ladies to get them out of their panties. Still playing the same old game you always have."

Her comments stung, an affront to the way he viewed himself. Sure, he loved women and enjoyed their company, but she insinuated something much more sinister behind his actions. He was always upfront and honest with his liaisons, clear he didn't want anything long term. Layla had been the one exception to that rule, knocking him off his game for six months—a short amount of time for the average couple, but practically the equivalent of years when Rashad considered the length of time he usually engaged the women he slept with.

"I'm not playing a game. You can pretend you don't care, but we both know you and I were great together."

"We had our moments, I'll give you that, but it's been almost three years—a long time, and you didn't call once." She met his gaze head on.

Guilty as charged. He'd pretended not to care, pretended her departure from his life was one of those things, but as the days turned into weeks and weeks into months, he came to appreciate her importance, and meaningless hookups continuously failed to fulfill him. He had intended to call or produce an excuse to visit D.C., anything to see her—but never followed through. Because *she'd* left, so he continued living life as usual. Dating, working, convinced he was over her no matter how many times she came to mind. Seeing her tonight made him wonder if all that had been a lie.

"Not because I didn't care."

"Mhmm. Well, I've moved on." She gently but firmly extricated her arm from his grip.

"You seeing someone now?"

Layla lips tilted up at the corners, the wry smile and seductively narrowed eyes giving nothing away. "That's none of your business."

"I'm making it my business."

"Why do you care?"

"You told me you'd think about it, and then the next thing I knew, you called and broke up with me. No explanation. No chance for renegotiation."

"What would have been the point? You wanted to slow down. Those were your words. I gave you what you wanted."

"I didn't want *us* to end," he grated.

"Ohhh, you wanted to continue seeing me on your terms. Well, sorry to disappoint you, honey," she said, patting his chest. "I have my own terms, too, and I wasn't interested."

"Have you been seeing someone?" He asked, a glutton for punishment, hating that he needed to know.

She watched him with a bit of a smirk on her lips. "Did you think I would be sitting around, twiddling my thumbs, waiting for you to want me again?"

"I never stopped wanting you," he said in a low, raw voice.

The words got to her because her lips parted, and his eyes tracked her gulp from the top of her neck to the base of her throat. She tucked her hair behind her ear, her nervous tick giving him a sense of satisfaction because it meant she was not nearly as indifferent to him as she pretended to be.

If nothing else, he knew she wanted him by the fire in her eyes and the way her hungry gaze ate him up. She would fight him every inch of the way, however, simply to prove a point.

"I'm not naïve enough to believe that your desire for me means you've been sleeping alone, and certainly not for almost three years. You shouldn't be naïve, either," she said.

The thought of her clawing another man's sheets and sobbing *his* name was enough to make him want to punch the wall, but he maintained his calm.

"Whoever the lucky bastard is, maybe I should put him on notice."

"Why?"

"Now that I know you're in town, his days are numbered."

Her lips tightened, but the heat of desire banked in her eyes.

She tossed her head so that her black hair swished to the left in her signature move—which meant she was about to give him a piece of her mind. Sweet-natured Layla had a sharp tongue when pushed too hard. But instead of a soul-slicing barb that cut him to pieces, her lips paused in an open position, and her gaze drifted to a point beyond his shoulder as if someone had caught her eye.

Almost at the same time, a hand touched his shoulder. Rashad didn't have to turn around to know Natasha was standing behind him. She came up beside him, wearing a friendly smile on her face.

"Hi," she said, looking between them.

A flash of—hurt?—filled Layla's eyes. *Dammit.* Natasha's appearance had reversed what little progress he'd made, which hadn't been much at all. He'd conveyed the message loud and clear to Layla that he still wanted her, but Natasha's appearance had the potential to make him look like a liar. A game player, like she thought him to be.

Her lips expanded into an equally friendly smile. "Hi, I'm Layla."

"I'm Natasha."

"Nice to meet you." Her gaze lifted to Rashad. No emotion in her eyes, only a cool exterior that was in direct contrast to the passionate woman he knew her to be. "It was good to see you again, Rashad. I have to go. Take care."

She glided away—back straight, steps fluid and graceful. If not for the silver high heels that played peekaboo with the hem of her flowy dress, one could easily believe that she was floating on air instead of walking across the floor. She took her position at Ethan's side, once again rejoining the conversation she abandoned earlier, and the absence of her presence unearthed an unexpected longing. Layla Fleming had rocked his world on many occasions, and right now he was hard-pressed to recall why he'd wanted to slow down.

"Who is she?" Natasha asked, following his line of sight.

"No one," Rashad muttered, but she wasn't no one.

He'd never met a woman he couldn't persuade to his point of view, until Layla. After six months together, he'd asked for them to slow down, and she walked away. Completely unexpected. And, apparently, she had lied to him.

No one was perfect, and he should accept that his previously perfect record had been tarnished. Losing Layla had been a one off.

But her dismissal and dishonesty not only piqued his interest, they challenged him in a way that caused an exhilarated tightening of his body. No person on earth loved a challenge more than he did, and he was determined to get her back into his bed.

Yes, there were other fish in the sea, but he wanted *this* fish.

He'd have to cancel with Natasha. No way he was sleeping with her tonight after that interaction with Layla.

Envious of the cling of the fabric that lay against her soft skin, his eyes didn't leave her rear view as he moved toward the exit with Natasha.

Dick hard. Fighting the urge to go get her.

3

Rashad's voice was distracting, all low and sexy. How did his clients concentrate on his counsel when he talked?

Layla tried to act normal, half-listening to the conversation around her. Smiling when they smiled. Laughing when they laughed so it wasn't obvious that she barely paid attention.

What a surprise. She'd never expected to stumble across Rashad at the event. She thought for sure she'd run into him somewhere mundane—like the supermarket or one of the restaurants they'd frequented. So much so, she'd stopped going to some of her favorite places to make sure she never saw him.

She became acutely aware of him, and what must be his date, leaving the venue. How dare he ask if she was seeing anyone when he'd come there with another woman? She bit down on her molars to stem the shaking that threatened to overtake her body.

Her eyes followed him and Natasha out the door. Rashad Greene. Phenomenal in bed, not so phenomenal out of it.

A well-formed man with skin that was dark brown, bordering on black, he oozed sex appeal with every action. His walk. His talk. His laugh. The way he scrubbed a hand across the low, fine beard on a jaw that looked strong and sharp enough to cut through marble.

Tall in stature, he had an arresting face, the kind that made you stop and stare against your will. His thick lips seemed almost indecent with their sensuality. When he was aroused, his broad nose quivered and his eyes—as dark as midnight—trailed lazily down her body as if he recognized his own power and reveled in it.

That's why she'd had to make a clean break. That's why she'd lied and pretended she was moving to D.C. The sexual tension between them practically crackled whenever they were together. Her wrist still felt warm where he'd touched her, and she regretfully acknowledged she had zero self-control when faced with the magnitude of Rashad Greene's midnight-colored eyes and seductive smile.

The men she'd dated since their break up—Devin, Chance, and most recently, Elijah—had all been inadequate substitutes for the man who made her blood heat with one lazy smile. Being with him was like having a best friend she couldn't keep her hands off of. She'd missed him, at first. As time went on, she realized with a sinking heart that he wouldn't call, which meant he didn't miss her the way she missed him. That's when she resolved to put Rashad and all memories of him out of her mind.

"I'm ready to go," Ethan said in her ear.

His voice snapped Layla into the present.

"Sounds good to me," she said.

She and Ethan said goodbye and made their way out of the room. Layla picked up her mink stole at the coat check, and on the way to the front door, she pulled her cell phone from the pocket of her dress and called the chauffeur to let him know to meet them out front.

"Big plans this weekend?" Ethan asked as he scrolled through his phone.

"Nothing major. Grocery shopping and laundry. That's about it."

They stepped outside, and she inhaled the dewy February air, cooler from the gently falling rain.

"Who was the guy you went off with? I didn't recognize him." As a real estate developer, Ethan prided himself on knowing people and had an uncanny ability to never forget a face or name.

"No one important. An old friend, that's all." Layla kept her voice casual.

"Your reaction to seeing him suggested he's more than an old friend," Ethan remarked.

He was way too perceptive, and she'd been working with him for five years, so he'd come to know her well, like she'd come to know him.

"He's my ex. Rashad," she admitted.

Ethan's brow wrinkled as he concentrated. "The one you broke up with a few years ago?"

"Yes."

"Was this the first time you've seen each other since then?"

"Yes."

"Running into him must have been surprising."

"Very," Layla admitted.

Ethan didn't ask any more questions. They were not close enough for him to pry any deeper into her feelings and thoughts about her private life.

The black limo sidled up to the curb, and the driver, Halston, hopped out wearing a black uniform and cap. He was middle-aged, with a scar that ran from his left cheek to the center of the side of his neck. Ethan had hired him because he was a former Navy Seal and for that reason doubled as a bodyguard. He opened the door, and they both slid into the back.

During the ride to Layla's loft, they talked a little about tonight's event, and then Ethan focused on the phone, following up on messages left on his voicemail. She didn't pay too much attention to his conversations because they were mostly business-related, and he was very rigid about the separation of his work and personal life. His executive assistant handled his work calendar and business issues, while Layla concentrated on his personal calendar and personal tasks—like managing his household, picking up his dry cleaning, and making sure important people in his life received the appropriate gifts on their birthdays and special occasions.

She joined his staff after being bored as a legal secretary, and while looking for more exciting work, she learned about the opportunity with Ethan. After working for two demanding attorneys, anticipating the needs of one man didn't pose much of an issue.

Though supportive, her parents hadn't been thrilled by her career decisions. They'd expected her to go into law like her other siblings—three of whom worked at the family law firm and two of whom had gone into local politics. Much preferring the supportive role, Layla knew that path wasn't for her.

Ethan could be demanding at times, particularly when he was in a bad mood, but overall she enjoyed her job. She had great benefits, a six-figure salary, and nice perks that included trips to exotic locations, hefty bonuses, expensive gifts, and free use of a loft in an exclusive part of town.

When they arrived at her building, Halston came around with an umbrella and opened the door.

"Good night, Ethan. I'll see you on Monday," Layla said.

He waved distractedly, deeply engrossed in a phone conversation. She didn't take offense. She'd worked with him enough to know that he wasn't being rude, he was busy.

Halston escorted her to the door, and after a quick goodbye, she made her way up to her loft. Inside, she kicked off her heels and slipped out of the dress Ethan instructed a local boutique to send over for tonight's event. Another perk. Whenever she accompanied him to an event, he made sure she didn't have to pay for a single item needed to prepare.

After washing off her makeup and brushing her teeth, she crawled into bed but couldn't sleep. Not with Rashad on her mind. The image of his face gnawed at her and kept her unduly restless after a long day that should result in a night of fitful sleep.

She stared up at the high ceiling, crisscrossed with exposed pipes and wood beams. She wanted to call one of her best friends to tell them she'd seen Rashad tonight but decided to wait until tomorrow.

To her, Rashad was still an enigma. He remained closed off, sharing very little about his past, while she'd been an open book. He had a way of pulling information out of you while revealing nothing about himself. Perhaps that had hurt the most. That he didn't want to share his life with her beyond spending the night at each other's house and dating. She was never allowed to get past the surface with him.

He knew all about her big family of three brothers and two sisters, and how difficult leaving the D.C. area had been when she decided to move to Atlanta. All she knew was that his parents died when he was young, causing him to spend time in foster care. He'd also started a financial investment firm, Newmark Advisors, with his best friend, Alex.

Six months together, and she never really knew him. Nothing had made that clearer than when he suggested the new terms of their relationship. To go from spending the bulk of their free time together, to being relegated to what she considered a booty call, had been devastating. She kept wondering what she'd done wrong. She'd thought they were heading toward a long-term relationship, while he'd been secretly plotting a way out.

With her wounded pride and damaged heart barely intact, she eventually turned him down. A week into his constant phone calls, she lied and said she was moving back to D.C. The calls stopped, and though she'd gotten her wish, the immediate lack of interest hurt like she'd never experienced before. Clearly, if she were no longer sexually available to him, he was not interested.

Tonight, he hadn't denied not trying to call her, which meant he didn't know she had changed her phone number, which more than anything confirmed he'd only cared about sex. If he'd cared about her as a person, surely he would have reached out to her at least once. Heaven knew she had wanted to reach out to him multiple times but hadn't, simply to maintain her sanity. Now she was doubly glad she hadn't. She would have been the only one making an attempt at reconciliation because Rashad simply hadn't cared.

Layla burrowed deeper under the duvet. Seeing him had certainly rattled her, but the Atlanta metro area consisted of over eight thousand square miles and over six million people. She didn't expect to run into him again anytime soon.

4

Layla stuffed her feet in a pair of Nike tennis shoes and zipped up her jacket. In the bathroom, she pulled her hair into a ponytail and left the warmth of her loft for a walk in the cold to her favorite neighborhood spot, Coffee Cup. She'd become a regular almost from the time she moved into the loft. The brisk walk was a way to get in some early morning exercise, and treating herself to breakfast was a simple way to pamper herself.

The entire neighborhood was conducive to walking, with a market nearby and plenty of small, locally owned eateries that served tapas, sandwiches, and other types of meals. Overall, her favorite was Coffee Cup because they served excellent coffee, and their breakfast and lunch were unmatched.

Strolling down the sidewalk, she allowed the fresh air to revive her, and though she tried not to think about her interaction with Rashad the night before, she couldn't get him out of her mind. How had he been the past few years? Who was Natasha, the woman he was with? How important was she to him?

A prick of pain needled her chest, and Layla pushed her way inside the shop with a little more force than necessary. She nodded a greeting at one of the servers, the owner's eldest daughter. Taking her place in line, she scoured the menu board behind the counter, and when her turn came, she greeted Brent, the owner's son.

His big grin welcomed her like always. "Hey, Layla. How's it going this morning?"

"Pretty good."

"Let's see... I'm guessing you'll have a large coffee, a blueberry muffin, and a whole wheat bagel with cream cheese, smoked salmon, and dill."

"Did you have to call me out like that?" she asked with a laugh. No matter how many times she looked at the menu, she always ordered the same thing. "One of these days I'm going to switch up my order."

"I'm still waiting for that day," Brent said, punching keys on the register. "By the way, I made sure to keep your favorite table empty."

Layla leaned across the metal counter and whispered, "I told you that you don't have to do that."

"I don't care," Brent whispered back.

They both laughed, with her shaking her head, and then she paid for the meal. He was too nice, but she appreciated that he looked out for her. Sometimes the shop could get really full and there would be nowhere to sit, or she'd get stuck sitting at a table in the middle of the dining room, which she hated. The table he'd secured for her with a *Reserved* sign was in a corner where she could look out at the street.

Later, she slowly ate her meal while scrolling through the financial app on her phone, happy to see her portfolio was performing nicely. She'd have to thank Ethan for the stock tips he'd given her a month ago. As a financial advisor, Rashad used to give her a lot of advice, but now she—

"Stop it," Layla muttered. She'd made a promise to herself that she wouldn't get caught up thinking about Rashad or the past and needed to keep it.

After finishing her meal, she left a generous tip before waving and leaving for the short walk back to her place. She was halfway home when she saw Rashad exiting a yellow Porsche illegally parked at the curb. A sports car, flashy like him. He used to own a red one, and when she pointed out that type of vehicle didn't seem like a financially prudent purchase, he said everyone needed to have a toy, and it brought him pleasure. He more than made up for the indulgence by being smart about other investments of his money.

Her footsteps slowed, and when his gaze landed on her face, her heart stuttered. Somehow, she remained in motion, on autopilot rather than with any real sense of what she was doing.

Rashad strolled toward her, the epitome of big-dick energy, and he never looked more so than when he was dressed casually, like now. He wore a pair of gray sweatpants and a dark blue Henley that showed off his defined chest and arms. His sexy, swaggerlicious stride turned heads, and his mannerisms conveyed he was not only good in bed, he could make you forget all others while you wept tears of ecstasy. She knew because it had happened to her.

"Mind if I walk with you?" he asked.

"Yes."

He fell into step beside her anyway, undeterred by her frosty reception.

"What are you doing here?" Layla asked, keeping her eyes on the sidewalk in front of them.

"I knew I'd find you this morning. You're a creature of habit, and I see nothing's changed. I thought about joining you for breakfast, but I know how much you like your Saturday morning ritual, so I decided to wait until you finished eating."

"How nice of you," Layla said sarcastically.

"You still having a large coffee, a blueberry muffin, and a whole wheat bagel with cream cheese, smoked salmon, and dill?"

Layla came to an abrupt stop. She really needed to change up her choices. Next week for sure. "What's the point of reciting what I like to eat, Rashad?"

"You're the same, Layla. Nothing's changed—except your phone number."

"You finally called."

"Yes. Last night you didn't mention that your number had changed."

"If you'd cared to call before, you would have known that," she pointed out.

Rashad nodded. "Fair enough. Can we start over?"

Crossing her arms, Layla asked, "Start what over, exactly?"

"The conversation from last night."

"I thought I made myself clear that I'm not interested in pursuing another relationship or whatever it is you're interested in."

"I'm interested in friendship," he said.

"Oh, right. You want to be friends," Layla said, voice dripping with sarcasm.

She started moving again, walking faster this time to escape him and this conversation she didn't want to have. His long legs easily kept stride with hers, exerting little effort, as if he were out for a leisurely stroll.

"You sound like you don't believe me," Rashad said.

"That's because I don't. You're only interested in one thing."

"How exactly did you come to that conclusion?"

Layla side-eyed him. "Past experience is the best indicator of future performance."

Rashad grabbed her arm, and the warmth of his fingers seared her skin through the lightweight jacket. She wanted to yank away, but couldn't. He was touching her again, like last night. The memory of his fingers around her wrist was as vivid as the fingers wrapped around her arm right now.

"And you don't miss it?" he asked.

"Miss what?"

Rashad backed her against the brick wall of a building, not

caring they were in the middle of the street with the occasional pedestrian walking by.

Eyes boring into hers, his voice dropped. "You know what."

Layla's belly quivered, denial burning on the tip of her tongue, but she couldn't speak the lie. Of course she missed it, them. The way they used to be together.

Rashad's lovemaking skills were unmatched, and they used to damn near burn up the bed when they made love. She could never get enough of him, and whenever they went too long without seeing each other, she ached until she could see him, touch him, press her body against his.

Instead of answering, she tilted her chin higher. "Is that why you came here? To see if I missed *it*?"

"I came here to see you, but I am curious about that part." His nostrils flared for a split second before he shook his head and let out a deep breath. "Shit. Let's try again. Contrary to what you believe, I do care. So tell me, how have you been, Layla?"

She dropped her gaze and had a sudden urge to burst into tears. She shook off his hand. How could such a simple question make her feel so weepy? How could he so easily break down her tough girl act and make her feel vulnerable and helpless with a few words of interest?

"Fine," she replied. She lifted her gaze again, and he continued to stare at her with concern in his eyes.

"And your family?"

"Fine. How about you?"

"Been better. Miss my friend. Miss my lover."

"Don't."

"Why?"

"Because…"

He waited.

"Because a clean break is what I wanted."

"I know, and you got that clean break, right? You lied and pretended you were moving to D.C."

Layla opened her mouth to deny the accusation, but he briefly lifted a finger to quiet her.

"Don't deny it. We both know it's true."

She fell silent and gazed at a couple across the street. The man had his arm around the woman, and they were laughing as they walked and talked. They looked so happy. That used to be her and Rashad, before he asked to downgrade their relationship.

"I understand why you did it. Because we were intense, and if we kept in touch, you'd give in to me again."

"You're overestimating your appeal."

"That's not what the little pulse right here says." He lifted a finger to her neck, and she slapped away his hand.

"You have a very high opinion of yourself."

"But am I right?"

With a heated glower, she refused to admit her weakness for him. "Believe it or not, you can't get everything you want, Rashad."

He tilted his head to the side. "Since when?" Raw arrogance took over his body, and the mocking light in his eyes set her teeth on edge. As far as he was concerned, nothing was beyond his reach if he worked hard enough.

"Since *now*."

"I'd believe that if you didn't lie about remaining in Atlanta. You were afraid if we saw each other, I could have you."

His gaze strolled down her body, and her cheeks heated. She looked anything but sexy in the jacket, joggers, and tennis shoes, but by the way his eyes were eating her up, you'd think she was standing before him in lacy lingerie. Perhaps that's what he was imagining. He bought her sexy lingerie a couple of times, and she'd loved modeling the pieces for him as he leaned back on his elbows, eyes dark and hungry with male appreciation.

"Have me, like a piece of meat?" Layla asked with an arched eyebrow, determined to win this battle of wills.

"Don't make the comment ugly. You know what I mean."

"Maybe I didn't want to see you."

Rashad smirked. "Nah, that's not it."

Her lips firmed, and she flexed her fingers, itching to smack the smirk off his face. Averting her eyes again, she let the stony silence speak on her behalf.

"Layla."

Her jaw tightened as she fought the barrage of emotions that came from him whispering her name.

"I messed up, but I miss you like crazy. That's the truth."

He spoke in a voice that she'd never heard before and wasn't accustomed to. Even more unnerving were the words he'd said. *He'd missed her?* Rashad didn't talk about feelings or share his innermost thoughts. He wasn't the type to bare his soul and certainly wasn't the type to admit he missed *her*. How was she supposed to fight against all of this?

She returned her attention to him and wished she hadn't. It was so unfair how absolutely beautiful he was, with his perfect features and perfect skin and perfect... everything. He was made to seduce women. Even his laugh was seductive—smooth, throaty, with a sparkle in his eyes that matched the diamond earrings in each ear.

"I lied. I don't want to be your friend." He braced his hands on either side of her shoulders, and her heart started to race in panicked excitement. She knew what he was about to do.

"Don't," Layla said.

"Don't what?"

"Kiss me."

"If I thought you meant that, I wouldn't." He spoke in a low, gruff voice, one that she'd heard before and was accustomed to.

"Stop," she whispered weakly, shrinking into the wall as far as she could.

He followed, his mouth stopping a hairsbreadth from hers, nostrils flaring. "I can't."

When his lips touched hers, her resistance melted away. She'd never stood a chance. That's why distance between them was essential.

Rashad kept his hands on the brick behind her. The only parts of their bodies that touched were their lips. He coaxed her mouth into a deeper kiss with gentle pressure and the teasing tip of his tongue.

Her hands moved of their own volition, sliding over his hard chest, taking delight in molding the contours of his lean waist and hard abs.

Kissing him was heaven. Bliss. Her mouth softened, and she allowed his tongue entrance to explore the innermost areas of her mouth. Layla moaned, shivering not from the cold but from the desire rushing through her blood. She was burning up, achy, like someone in the middle of a hot flash. Her fingers clutched the Henley as she stepped closer to his heat, the tips of her breasts grazing his firm chest.

Rashad abruptly wrenched his mouth from hers and expelled a deep breath. Layla whimpered her disapproval and tightened her grip on his shirt, resting her forehead against his collarbone, right beneath his chin.

"Step back, Layla." His voice shook.

With a deep swallow, she reluctantly stepped back into the wall.

Rashad's eyes bored into hers. "I want to fuck you so bad—right here, in the middle of the fucking street, and I don't care who sees."

She trembled at the rawness of his words. His arms were still stretched out on either side of her shoulders, but beneath the shirt his muscles were corded with tension. In fact, his entire body was rigid, but his chest heaved up and down with the energy he exerted to keep control.

"You're a good woman, Layla. Any man would be lucky to have you. That's why I'm here. I want to be that man. Will you give me another chance?"

She swallowed past the lump in her throat. She didn't want to answer while she wasn't thinking straight.

Rashad pressed a kiss to her forehead, and she briefly closed her eyes, clenching her fists to keep from reaching for him again.

He stepped back and smiled at her. Not one of his cocky grins, but an achingly sweet smile that twisted her heart into knots.

"You need time to think. My number hasn't changed. Call me in a week if you think we have a chance."

As Rashad walked away, Layla felt an invisible line tugging her toward him, but she resisted and turned her back on him.

"No," she whispered.

She rushed to her building on shaky knees and took the elevator to her loft. Inside, she flopped onto the bed and buried her face in the pillows. Hating him. Hating herself. Hating that between her thighs was wet and throbbing.

Will you give me another chance?

She knew what the answer should be. No. That's it.

But her beating heart insisted she choose the other option. Because the ache—the unbearable need for him—had returned.

5

After dinner laughter filled the living room of Rashad's friend and business partner, Alex Barraza. His wife, Sherry, who also worked at the company, sat on the chair opposite, next to Alex. The couple married six months ago, in August.

They'd both been crazy about each other from the moment Sherry started at Newmark Advisors. In the beginning, neither had acted on the very powerful attraction between them. Rashad was glad they'd finally worked out the secret Alex had been keeping from her. Sherry was a good woman, and her relationship with Alex had brought Rashad closer to her, as well.

Sherry, whose light brown skin always glowed like she'd recently come out of the sun, placed a hand on Alex's thigh. "I'm feeling kind of tired, so I'm going to leave you two alone and head to bed. Rashad, you have to give me the recipe for your coffeecake."

"I'll email it to you when I get home. I found the recipe online but tweaked it a little bit and added my own secret ingredients."

"Yes, I get to know the secret ingredients." Sherry rubbed

28

her hands together, which elicited a laugh from both men. "Can't wait. Have a good night."

"Good night," Rashad returned.

As Sherry stood, Alex's fingers held onto hers, their touch lingering. Tonight they'd shared their great news with him. Sherry was three months pregnant, which wasn't obvious yet and easily hidden beneath her loose-fitting blouse.

After she slipped from the room, Alex said, with amusement in his eyes, "She'll be out later after you're gone to finish off the rest of the cake. She was being polite earlier."

Rashad chuckled.

Alex was not only his closest friend, he considered him a brother. They'd known each other since they started college at eighteen, bonding over the fact that neither had any close family they could depend on. Alex had traveled from Colombia to attend school in the States, and Rashad had more or less been fending for himself for a large portion of his life.

Forced to grow up fast, a stint in foster care taught him that he was better off on his own, and by the time he was sixteen, he lived alone, renting a room in a boarding house while working part-time and going to school. In college he met Alex, and they formed their own family with a third member—Heather. He still missed her, but she was in a better place now.

Back when they'd been roommates, Alex would do the cooking and Rashad baked. He learned to bake from his foster mother and was really good at it. People saw the finished product as art, but for him the best part was in the creation. The need for precision in baking made him concentrate and had a calming effect, something his foster mother had noticed early on. So she'd continued to teach him, and he'd found a hobby that not only filled his belly but calmed him when he was upset.

"Can I get you anything else to drink?" Alex asked in accented English, eyeing Rashad's empty bottle of beer on the table beside him.

"No, I'm good. What's the word on Lion Mountain Vineyards?"

Rashad had been the one to suggest they start Newmark Advisors, and now they were likely on the cusp of another business venture—one that Alex had suggested.

Alex sat forward, his hazel eyes brightening with excitement. "They're not going to let anyone know they're selling the place for at least a few more months, so we have time."

The owners of Lion Mountain Vineyards were retiring, but neither of their two children were interested in taking over, which presented an unexpected opportunity for Alex and Rashad.

Alex and Sherry had visited the award-winning Georgia winery several times, and on one of those visits his friend learned about the owners' desire to sell. Though neither he nor Rashad had any experience in wine-making, they believed they could manage the property as long as the employees remained, which by all indications they planned to.

"Excellent. That gives us time to do a little research and get our finances together."

Alex nodded. "When can you get up there?"

"Not for a few weeks, at least."

With tax season coming up, a lot of their clients were reaching out for ways to maximize tax advantage savings by contributing more to their IRAs and 401k's. Newmark Advisors was also busy providing information about trading losses and gains from the previous year for clients not savvy enough to download the data from the company site themselves.

"They don't know me, so I'll go up there as a customer and check the place out."

"Good idea, but I'm sure you'll like it. Might be the kind of place you can take one of your women," Alex teased.

Rashad gave a short laugh and brushed imaginary lint from his jeans. He was used to being teased about his reputation as a ladies' man, but tonight the joke didn't quite land because he wasn't in the mood for that kind of ribbing. Not after what happened between him and Layla last week.

Concerned eyes trained on Rashad's face, Alex asked, "What's wrong with you?"

"What do you mean?"

"Come on, it's me. You've been off this week, and tonight too. It's Friday night and you're eating dinner at the home of your married friends."

"We haven't hung out in a while outside of work," Rashad said with a shrug.

Alex didn't say a word. He simply sat in silence and waited, and Rashad laughed. If anyone knew him, it was Alex.

"Okay, fine, you're right. Maybe I have been a little bit off, but I thought I was covering it well." Knees to elbows, he told Alex, "I saw Layla last week. Twice." Alex and Layla had met once, when she showed up at the Newmark Advisors office.

"She's in town?"

"She never left."

Alex's eyebrows lifted in surprise.

Suddenly restless, Rashad stood up from the chair and paced to the bookcase that spanned an entire wall. He spun around and went into detail about the first night at the silent auction and told Alex about how he had gone to Layla's favorite breakfast spot the next day.

"Remind me, why did you break up?" Alex asked.

Rashad shrugged. "Things were getting too serious, and you know I don't do serious. I told her we needed to slow down."

"Oh yes, that's right. You got scared."

Rashad stiffened. "I wouldn't use the word scared."

"What word would you use?" Alex asked.

"I'd say... I was uncomfortable."

"So you were uncomfortable, and you told her you wanted to slow down, and she broke up with you."

"Yes, which I think was pretty drastic."

"Or maybe she was scared—excuse me, uncomfortable too."

Rashad knew Alex was being sarcastic, but he'd simply needed breathing room because his desire to spend time with Layla had become borderline obsessive. His every thought, his every action, had been consumed with her. Would Layla like this? Would Layla like to come with him to this event? If he thought about buying a piece of furniture, he felt the need to consult her first. That wasn't normal.

On the outside he seemed good-natured and happy-go-lucky. On the inside, he was always waiting for the other shoe to drop and rob his life of whatever pleasure he'd foolishly indulged in. So, no attachments. No long-term relationships. He preferred to keep his affairs as affairs—short term and casual so no one got hurt—especially him. But Layla had been different. She'd forced him to consider permanence, a future—an abomination in his world.

Plus, she was so darn... kind and considerate. One day she popped up at his office unannounced, bringing him a drink and a Reuben sandwich on rye because they'd chatted on the phone twenty minutes before, during which he'd mentioned he didn't have time to get a bite to eat. For her, the gesture had been no big deal—thoughtful and typical of her. She was loyal to a fault, and if you needed a favor, she was the one person to ask and trust she'd come through.

But when she showed up at his office with lunch, warning bells had blared, and he knew he had to pump the brakes on the speeding train of their relationship. He'd managed to keep her from getting too close, doling out very little information about himself, but that day she'd met Alex, one of the most important people in his life. She'd breached his veneer of privacy, and that was a no-no.

Yet, here he was, playing a waiting game. He wanted to give Layla space and let her come to him, but tomorrow would make a week since he walked away from her on the street. He could still taste her. He could still smell the freshness of her skin after her morning shower. How was he supposed to handle this need for her? After almost three years he'd been certain he succeeded, but just the sight of her at the auction had sent him spiraling into unprecedented yearning for a few moments of her time.

"I should have called her." That was his biggest regret. He had a feeling if he had called, just once, that would've made a difference in her reception to him when they ran into each other.

Alex nodded but didn't say a word. Both he and Heather had advised Rashad to call, but he hadn't heeded their advice.

"You gave her a week. It hasn't been a week yet," Alex pointed out.

"Damn near," Rashad muttered.

She wanted him, of that he was certain. She kissed him with the same energy that he kissed her. Would that be enough?

Alex ran his fingers through his hair, a sure indication that he was about to say something Rashad wouldn't like. "It's going to take time to convince Layla to get back involved with you. Think about your breakup from her point of view. For months the two of you were going along fine, spending a lot of time together. Then one day you decide that you want to slow down."

"I understand that, but I didn't want our relationship to end," Rashad said defensively.

As he strolled back to the chair, his phone rang. He picked it up from the table beside the empty bottle of beer. Not recognizing the number, he intended to ignore it, but at the last second decided to answer.

"Hello?"

"Hi, Rashad." Layla.

His eyes found Alex's, and he pointed to the phone. *It's her,* he mouthed.

"Do you have a minute?" she asked.

"Sure." A minute. An hour. Ten hours. He had however much time she needed.

"I've been thinking about what you said last week, and I've

decided that you're right. We are good together. Explosively good."

Stunned, all Rashad could get out was one word. "Okay."

"I want to start seeing you again."

"Okay," he said again. *Hell yeah!*

"Could we meet sometime, when you're free?"

"I'm free right now," he said, picking up his keys.

"You want to meet tonight?" She sounded surprised.

"Yes. How about that tapas place near your loft in fifteen minutes?" He couldn't wait to see her. Excitement was already beating through his blood.

"I'm not at home. I'm in the car. I left Ethan's a few minutes ago."

"I'm not at home, either. I'm at Alex's. Want to meet somewhere else?"

"Um, sure. How about that restaurant in Decatur, the one that serves the strong drinks and has outdoor seating?"

"Eli's?"

"Yes."

"I can meet you at the bar in thirty minutes," Rashad said.

"Okay, I'll see you then."

He hung up. Unable to help himself, he grinned, harder than he had in a week. "Looks like your boy is back in play after all. She wants to meet and talk about us getting back together."

"She said that?" Alex said, sounding and looking surprised.

"Pretty much."

"That's great."

"Yeah. I better get out of here. Wish me luck."

"*Buena suerte*," Alex said as Rashad rushed through the door.

✼ 6 ✼

Sipping a cosmopolitan at the bar, Layla waited impatiently for Rashad to arrive. Though she hadn't anticipated having this conversation so soon, on the ride to the restaurant she ran through how to present her idea to him in a matter-of-fact manner.

Still, she was nervous. Her call to him had been impulsive, and she wished she'd had a chance to discuss her decision in detail with her girlfriends, but Rashad's request to meet tonight had taken her by surprise and squashed her decision to wait. That was probably for the best. She needed to get this done, and besides, she didn't think he'd turn her down.

When Rashad arrived, her gaze lingered on his long legs in worn jeans and the span of his shoulders beneath a striped sweater.

"Hi," she said.

"Hi." He sat down and twisted so they were facing each other, one arm resting on the bar.

It was late, and most of the guests were in the dining room, so the bar was fairly quiet and conversation would be easy. Only one guy sat on a stool at the end, looking like he was drowning his sorrows in the beer before him. A couple sat with their heads bent together at one of the bistro tables.

The bartender came over, a lively blonde with a ring in her nose. "What can I get for you?" she asked Rashad.

"Coke, light ice," he replied.

"A Coke?" Layla said, raising her eyebrows in surprise.

"I already had a few drinks at Alex's."

The bartender placed a glass with a straw in front of Rashad.

"How is he?"

She was simply making polite conversation because she didn't know Alex well and met him only one time, when she stopped by their office. Rashad had talked about Alex to her, so she'd been excited when she ran into both of them in the lobby of Newmark Advisors and Rashad introduced them. Unfortunately, she'd gotten the distinct impression that he hadn't wanted them to meet. He'd come across hesitant and brisk, and had all but shoved her into the elevator after thanking her for lunch. She'd said goodbye, feeling as if she'd overstepped her bounds, crushed that once again he was obviously shutting her out of part of his life.

"Fine. He got married."

"Really?"

"Yeah. Sherry, from the office."

"She's one of your financial advisors, right?" She vaguely remembered him mentioning her name before.

He nodded, his eyes trained on her face.

Layla took a swallow of her drink, taking solace in the effect of the cool liquid wetting her parched tongue. She'd expected the small talk to break the tension between them, but instead it placed a strain on the air and raised the temperature in the room.

"Well, I guess we better get to the reason why we're here," she said, tucking a strand of hair behind her left ear.

"You don't have to feel awkward or nervous, Layla. We know

each other, and we can go slowly, if you like—ease back into the relationship."

Oh boy, she better hurry up and explain what exactly she had in mind before he said anymore.

"Actually, that's what I want to talk to you about—the terms of our new relationship."

Frown lines appeared in his brow. "Terms?"

"Yes. It's true that I wanted to meet with you about us getting back together. I haven't been able to stop thinking about the kiss we shared the other day."

"Me, either." His voice dropped low and melted over her like warm honey, heat sparking in his eyes.

Layla rushed on before he got carried away. "The sex was always—"

"Spectacular."

Her inner thighs tightened, and she laughed softly. "Yes, that would be one way of describing it."

"You disagree?"

"Honestly, no. Which is why I called you." She nervously licked her lips. "Rashad, I'm not interested in being your girl-friend again, but you're right, I do miss... *it*."

His face blanked.

"If you're not seeing anyone, and I'm not seeing anyone, maybe we could... hook up every now and again," Layla said.

He blinked, coming out of the temporary daze cast by her words. "You mean like... fuck buddies?"

"That's a crude way of saying it, but, yes," Layla answered, shifting in her chair.

His eyes narrowed a fraction. "Are you messing with me?"

"No, I'm not," she assured him. True enough, a purely sexual relationship was outside her character, but he didn't have to act so surprised.

"You're serious?" he asked.

"Yes. What's wrong with my idea? You've done this before, haven't you?"

"Yes, but not with—" He stopped abruptly and chugged some Coke. Then he set down the glass. "I've had casual sexual partners before, no doubt, but I thought this conversation was going in a different direction."

"Maybe I should have told you what I was thinking when I called, but it didn't feel right making my offer over the phone. I hope you don't feel like I brought you here under false pretenses."

He kept his gaze on her as he twisted the glass on the bar top. "Not at all."

His gaze dropped to the round neckline of her blouse. She was completely covered, yet he looked at her as if she were partially undressed.

"So, do you accept, or do you need time to think about it?"

Rashad sat back. "I don't need time. The answer is yes."

Layla released a relieved breath, suddenly very aware of how much she'd wanted him to agree despite believing that he would.

"Good," she continued. "If we do this, we need some rules." Settling into the idea, she spoke calmly, as if they were discussing the weather.

"Let's hear them."

"First of all, we're not dating. This isn't a repeat of our previous relationship, and I want to make that clear. We're seeing each other until we each meet someone else that we're more compatible with."

Rashad rubbed a hand over his jaw as he mulled her words. "Okay."

"No spending the night at each other's house."

"Come on, now."

"Sleeping over promotes intimacy, which promotes feelings. Remember, this is sex-only."

"What if it's raining?"

"Get an umbrella."

"I'm talking about you. I wouldn't want you to go out in a

storm in the middle of the night when you could sleep at my place."

"I'll be fine, I won't melt," Layla said dryly.

His lips tightened with displeasure. "Anything else?"

"No calls after midnight. That's basically a booty call, and—"

"If we're entering a sex-only relationship, every call is a booty call."

"True, but late-night calls could lead to staying overnight, which means intimacy, and this is—"

"Yeah, yeah, I remember. Sex-only." He drained his glass and slammed it on the bar.

Clearing her throat, Layla asked, "Do you have any rules?"

He watched her in silence, and she fought the urge to squirm.

"One," Rashad said. "You're not allowed to screw anyone else while we're seeing each other."

She hadn't even considered sleeping with another man while with Rashad. He could more than satisfy her needs, but she didn't dare let him know her thoughts. He didn't need any more ego stroking.

"Not a problem. Neither are you," she said.

"Fine by me."

"Okay, well, I guess we're done here."

"I guess so."

Layla stood and reached into her purse, but before she could pay for her drink, Rashad also stood and dropped a few bills between their glasses.

As he towered over her in the tight space between the two stools, she drew a sharp breath.

"When?"

"When what?" She tipped her head back to gaze up into his black eyes. The two earrings glinted against his dark skin.

Rashad cupped her chin, the gentle hold wreaking havoc on her skin. Staring intently into her eyes, he asked, "When can I make love to you again?"

Layla almost melted on the spot.

"How about next weekend?" she suggested, her voice sounding tinny. "Because of Mother Nature, I'm out of commission for the next few days."

"Guess I'll have to wait until next weekend, then. Is the number you called me from your new number?"

"Yes."

"Good. Now I know how to reach you." Rashad bent his head and connected their lips.

The kiss was hard but gentle and prompted a soft whimper from her throat. She tasted the sweetness of the Coke and sweetness of his mouth. As his left arm circled her waist and his right hand cupped her jaw, heat slithered over her skin like a warm blanket. She took the liberty of resting her hand against his chest and letting her thumbnail scrape his nipple. It was his turn to groan, and she exulted in the sound, anticipating the moment in the not-too-distant future when she could see him lose complete control.

Rashad didn't make much noise when they made love, but when he came, it was a sight to behold. He cursed worse than a sailor, gritted his teeth, and pounded the bed when he climaxed. Watching him lose control was its own kind of aphrodisiac, and if not for being on her period, she'd go to his condo right now to watch the whole scene play out.

Rashad released her lips, and his warm breath kissed her throbbing mouth when he spoke. "I'll walk you out."

He escorted her to her white Cadillac SUV, which was parked on a side street.

Layla popped the locks and turned to face him. Under his watchful gaze, she tingled all over. "I'll call you."

"Do that."

He kissed her again, pressing her into the cool steel of the car. She found comfort in the steady beating of his heart against hers, and felt every inch of him—his chest, his powerful legs, and the hardness between his thighs.

Damn her period. Damn, damn, damn.

Rashad stepped back. "Good night."

"Good night," Layla replied breathlessly. She slid behind the wheel and drove off, shivering through the chills of excitement that rolled through her body.

RASHAD WATCHED LAYLA'S TAIL LIGHTS DISAPPEAR AROUND the corner, then he strolled to where his car was parked on the other side of the court house square.

Layla had changed, that was for sure. The woman who'd wanted commitment and asked him to share more of himself was now willing to have a purely sexual relationship. Shocking.

Unlike her, he'd had plenty of experience with those kinds of relationships, though he'd never had such a clinical discussion about the parameters before. In those types of arrangements, he typically juggled multiple sexual partners, as did the women he was involved with. They were open and honest, each person entering into the casual relationship with their eyes wide open. In Layla's case, he was not having that. He *couldn't*. Besides, she was more than enough to satisfy him.

He climbed into his Porsche and sat there for a minute, already anticipating having her back in his bed. Losing Layla Fleming had been the biggest mistake he'd ever made. He was pretty sure she was the only woman he'd come close to loving— as close as he could possibly come to romantic love.

Now he was about to have exactly what he wanted in the first place—Layla exclusively his without all the trappings of a serious relationship.

Rashad smiled as he started the car. The best of both worlds.

Life was good.

7

The bowling alley downtown contained a festive atmosphere, with blaring party music and groups of friends screaming and cheering each other on.

Layla tossed the ball down the alley, and as it veered left, she angled her body to the right, as if she could telepathically force it to go down the middle.

No such luck. The ball plopped into the gutter like the one before it. She didn't hit a single pin.

"Have you actually gotten worse?" Tamika, one of her best friends teased. She wore tight jeans with her short pixie styled in cute waves.

"Shut. Up," Layla said, holding her head high as she marched back to her seat.

Dana, her other best friend, giggled at their antics. Full-figured, with waist-length dreadlocks and two rings in her nose, she ate a late dinner of fries and chicken tenders at the table behind the chairs. Stabbing the fries, she dipped them in ketchup on the side of the plate.

"You're not much better," she told Tamika.

Tamika, headed to pick up a ball, curled one hand behind her back and shot Dana a backhanded bird. As Layla and Dana laughed, she picked up a ball at the return and then smoothly sent it rolling down the alley. It crashed into the pins and knocked over six of them.

Dana and Layla cheered and clapped while Tamika did a victory dance. With focused concentration, she took her second turn and knocked down an additional two pins. Despite Dana's teasing, Tamika ended the game as the winner, leading Dana by three points.

Dana tossed her empty plate into the trash and plopped down in front of the computer. "One more game?"

Tamika picked up her phone and checked the time, the diamond ring on her left hand picking up the overhead light. "Anton's playing pool with his friends until eleven, so I'm good for another hour. Then I'm going home to my *fiancé*."

"Do you have to say 'my fiancé' every time?" Dana asked.

In the chair next to Layla, Tamika glowed as she flashed a smile that extended from ear to ear. "Yes, because I like the sound of it."

Tamika and Anton had gotten engaged last fall and were actively house-hunting while also making preliminary plans for their wedding. The happy couple had gone through a rough patch but weathered the storm together, and their young relationship became stronger as a result.

Layla still hadn't told her girlfriends about her conversation with Rashad last night, but this lull in the game was the perfect time to do so. But first, she needed to update them on a personal matter.

"My dad started going to therapy last week, and so far so good. Mom said he's cranky but following the doctor's orders."

Her father had been sideswiped in traffic a while back, a scary situation that had prompted Layla to fly to D.C. while he was hospitalized. He'd undergone surgery for a broken collarbone, but once released had also been suffering from chronic pain and stiffness in his back, knees, and neck. Since he'd healed, he was supposed to start going to a physical therapist but constantly put it off. The discomfort had finally become too much to bear, and he'd succumbed to the urging of his family and the advice of his physicians.

"And Mrs. Fleming didn't have to put a gun to his head?" Dana asked in a dry tone.

Her friends knew how difficult her father could be. She'd talked about him often, plus they'd met him when they visited her family in D.C. As the head of a small but prestigious law firm he co-founded with his wife, Herschel Fleming craved control and couldn't function well without said control. He also had a well-documented aversion to doctors.

"No," Layla said with a laugh, "but I was planning to fly up there again and drag him to the doctor if he didn't. Luckily I don't have to."

"Thank goodness it didn't come to that, and if he listens to his therapist, he'll hopefully feel better soon," Dana said.

"What is it with men and doctors?" Tamika said.

"Hard-headed," Dana muttered. "Every one of them is like that. Omar's the same way. When he played football, he had no choice but to follow the team physicians' instructions, but now that he's retired, he acts like he's allergic to doctors. Last month I had to remind him to take his physical, again. I literally have the yearly appointment on my calendar because if I don't remind him, he won't go." She shook her head.

Silence.

"Hmm," Tamika said, tapping her lips.

"Hmm," Layla said too, tapping her chin.

Dana rolled her eyes and fought the smile at the corners of her mouth. "Guys, don't start."

"What do you mean?" Tamika asked, all wide-eyed and innocent.

"Omar and I are friends."

"We're friends, and I don't have a reminder set in my phone for either of you to go to the doctor," Layla said. "Do you have a reminder for my annual exam on your calendar, Tamika?"

"I sure don't. Do you have one for either of us, your *best* friends?" Tamika asked pointedly, to Dana.

"Enough. Can we please take the focus off me and my *friend*, Omar? Thank you." Dana swiveled in the chair and faced the monitor.

"Look at you, avoiding the issue. You date all these other men, and Omar is right there," Tamika said.

"I'm not avoiding the issue, I'm setting up the next game. Omar is a friend. How many times do I have to explain that?" Dana tapped the keyboard.

"Till we believe it," Layla quipped.

She and Tamika giggled while Dana shot them a dirty look.

"I have something to tell you guys," Layla announced.

"Sounds serious," Tamika turned in her direction.

Dana swung to face her, too, offering her full attention.

Her friends definitely wouldn't approve of her next remark because after her breakup with Rashad, she'd been very clear that she was done with him for good.

"I saw Rashad last night."

"Voluntarily?" Dana quirked an eyebrow.

"Yes."

"Um, why?" Tamika asked.

"Because I wanted to talk to him about getting back together."

Tamika's eyes widened.

"Layla—" Dana started.

Layla thrust up a hand. "Before you start, I already know what you're both going to say, believe me, and I agree. Rashad and I won't work. We've been there and done that. He's too closed off, but I realized that I don't need a normal relationship with him. I know exactly the kind of man he is, and I know what I'll tolerate. I intend to focus on the best part of our relationship, if you know what I mean."

"Yes, we know what you mean," Tamika said with a sly grin.

Layla blushed.

"I'm gonna need you to spell it out for me. What exactly are you thinking about doing with Rashad?" Dana asked.

Layla had no doubt that Dana knew exactly what she was suggesting, but being a practical person, she wanted Layla to explicitly state what she meant.

"I suggested we have a sexual relationship."

"You, Layla Fleming, are going to have a purely sexual relationship?" Dana asked with copious amounts of skepticism.

"Yes. I can absolutely do that," she said. "After all this time, I realize I don't want to be his girlfriend, and I don't want him as my boyfriend. However, what he lacked in the boyfriend department, he more than made up for in the bedroom."

"I don't think this is a good idea," Dana said.

"Why not? She's a grown woman and knows her own mind," Tamika said.

Dana shook her head. "Yes, she knows her own mind—"

"—I'm right here, guys. Please stop talking about me in the third person."

"You know your own mind, but you're not the type to go into a purely sexual relationship with anyone. You've never been that way. Tamika or me, yes. You, no. And with Rashad, of all people? The man who made you contemplate quitting your job because he was jealous of Ethan, your boss? The man who had you browsing bridal magazines and researching the meaning of baby names?"

Heat flamed Layla's cheeks at the embarrassing reminder that she'd been so into him, practically planning out the next thirty years of their lives while he'd been planning how to escape and move on to the next woman. "That was a long time ago," she said dismissively. "I know better now, and I've dated other men since then. It's not like I laid around the house pining for him."

Dana stared at her.

"Okay, fine, I pined for a couple of months, but then I recovered and moved on. I've been involved with three men since then, and Elijah was only a few months ago."

"Which didn't last. To be honest, I never thought you were truly invested in that relationship," Tamika said.

"I liked him, but he wasn't the one. That's all."

"And what about that guy you've been talking to? The one you met online?"

"I'm still going to talk to him. Rashad and I are only having sex, but we're allowed to see other people."

"I have to agree with Dana," Tamika said uneasily. "You know, and we know, that Rashad is your kryptonite. That was the whole reason for saying you were moving to D.C. You knew you couldn't handle him because he might wear you down."

"I can handle Rashad."

"Since when?" both friends asked at the same time.

"Thanks for the vote of confidence, but I have everything under control," Layla snapped. She'd prove to herself and to her friends that she was not as weak for Rashad as she used to be.

"R.I.P. your heart," Tamika muttered.

Layla gently elbowed her friend. "Thanks for believing in me."

"We don't want you to get hurt." Dana's eyes filled with worry.

"I've got this, you guys, really. I told you my plans because I want you to know. This time around, I only want one thing from Rashad, and that's sex." Saying it out loud made her feel stronger and more in control. "That's it. Nothing else."

🦋 8 🦋

L ayla entered Ethan's office carrying a large leather bag over her shoulder, his dinner, and a black suit she had picked up from the dry cleaner.

The office was literally the size of an apartment with plenty of windows and a private dining room and bathroom behind closed doors. The visible area was occupied by typical high-end executive office furniture, a conference room behind glass, and a sitting area for guests. The shades over the windows were currently drawn, blocking out the night and making the room seem extra quiet.

She placed the sack containing Ethan's dinner on the desk and turned to face him as he stormed through the door with a frown on his face.

"Thank goodness, you're here," he said, the lines in his forehead disappearing.

Layla handed over his change of clothes. "Halston is waiting for you downstairs," she said, as she unzipped the leather bag. "I've already made a phone call to the hotel and reminded them about your shellfish allergy. Daria and I touched base, and she reconfirmed your attorney will meet you at the airport for the flight out, and the ones in London will be there when you land and brief you on the ride to court."

In addition to his stateside attorney, an architect and another business associate would be joining Ethan on the transcontinental flight in his private jet so he could strategize before they landed. She hoped he took the opportunity to sleep on the plane, but knowing him, he'd be too wired. The man worked way too hard.

"Perfect. Could you stick around for a bit? I have a few more tasks to go over with you before I leave."

"Of course."

From the bag, Layla removed a box with his shoes and socks and a small case with the black Patek Philippe watch he always paired with his black suits. She followed him into the bathroom, placed the items on the counter, and then quickly exited.

While he showered, she unpacked his meal, drink, and utensils. Then she took a seat in front of his desk, in a plush burgundy chair that was one of only a few items with color in the room. Everything else was black or white. There were black and white photos on the wall of properties he owned, his desk was black and L-shaped, and the sitting area contained two black leather couches and the only other colorful furnishing in the room—a burgundy leather armchair.

Layla pulled her iPad from the bag at her feet and clicked on the appropriate notes app to get ready for their meeting. Ethan was going on a last-minute trip to London, one he wasn't pleased about because of its unexpectedness. Renovations had been stalled on one of his buildings for months. He'd let his people over there handle the problems, and today he'd learned there was a pending court case that he hadn't been informed about. Without a doubt, someone was getting fired.

That's why she was sitting in his office after nine at night but was accustomed to dealing with unexpected crises in working for him. While she waited for him to finish up, she replayed the other night with Rashad. The kiss, the way he held her, and her own reaction. Tingles shimmied from her breasts down to her inner thighs. She loved kissing him and would happily do it all the time if he'd let her.

Ethan exited the bathroom looking refreshed, fastening his cufflinks as he moved with powerfully graceful strides across the floor.

She came to her feet and straightened his tie. "Better," she said.

"Thank you."

As she watched him walk around the desk, she understood why Rashad had been concerned about their relationship. Ethan was a good-looking, virile, powerful man. Yes, she noticed all of that from day one when she interviewed with him, but not once during their five-year work relationship had he made an inappropriate comment or made a pass at her. In fact, he had a very low tolerance for that type of behavior from men in his position.

She essentially saw herself as his companion, except she got paid for the work. Her job was to make his life easier, and she did that by being efficient and anticipating his needs. For instance, tonight she brought him dinner, though he hadn't mentioned he hadn't eaten yet. She knew he sometimes skipped meals or ate unhealthy snacks when he was busy. Being that he was probably going to be preoccupied with meetings and phone calls on the plane, and when they landed he'd be thrown into more meetings, he needed some sustenance to continue performing at his peak.

He sat at the desk and while he ate went over a list of tasks he needed her to complete while he was out of town. Nothing too taxing, and all could be handled within a day, which meant she'd get a break while he was gone. When he finished the meal, he jumped up and grabbed his briefcase, looking around the room to make sure he hadn't forgotten anything.

"I'll see you when I get back," he said.

"Have a safe trip," Layla called after him.

She removed a cotton sack from the leather bag at her feet

and went into the bathroom. She tossed in Ethan's dirty clothes and then dropped the empty food containers in the trash. Turning out the light as she left the office, she headed to the elevator.

Once in the SUV, her phone rang, and Rashad's name flashed across the screen on the dashboard. Excitement thrummed in her veins. She'd intended to call him when she got home but was pleased to see he'd reached out to her.

"Hello?"

"What are you doing?"

Layla smiled through the biting of her lip. Good grief, she could barely contain her excitement.

"I just left Ethan's office. He's on his way overseas on a business trip."

"Does that mean you're free tonight?"

"Actually, it does."

"And Aunt Flo is gone?"

She smiled. "Yes, she is."

"It's before midnight. I want to see you. You want me to come to you, or will you come to me?"

Layla thought for a minute and then decided going to his home gave her leverage because she could leave whenever she wanted—as opposed to having to get him out of her apartment if he came to her.

"I'll come to your place, but I need to stop at Ethan's first to drop off a few things. Then I'll come over."

"The slave driver continues to slave drive even when he's not here, huh?"

"He's not bad, and I should have a few quiet days while he's gone."

Rashad grunted but didn't comment further. "How long before you get here?"

"Anxious, are you?"

He chuckled. "Maybe. How long?"

"Less than an hour. I'll call when I'm close."

"Do that. I'm waiting."

Layla pushed the speedometer higher on the way to Ethan's mansion. At first, she wasn't sure how this was going to work, but now she saw that it was completely possible for them to reignite their sexual relationship, and everything would be nice and uncomplicated.

They both knew what they were getting themselves into. Unlike last time, there would be no surprise conversations about slowing things down, and she was pleased that she hadn't completely capitulated to him. She'd created her own version of a relationship, one where she didn't have concerns about falling for Rashad again. Because she wouldn't. She saw through him now and knew he wasn't the man for her, but that didn't mean she couldn't enjoy herself in the search for Mr. Right.

Her stop at Ethan's lasted twenty minutes because she took a quick shower in one of the guest suites when she dropped off his personal belongings. Before leaving, she picked up two other suits that needed adjusting, which she'd take to his tailor first thing in the morning.

Back on the road, she called Rashad and let him know she was on her way. He gave her the password for the doorman, that way he'd send her right up when she arrived. She parked her car and then entered the lobby of the apartment building, and minutes later she was in the elevator, climbing to the eleventh floor.

Rashad opened the door before she knocked, which meant the doorman had alerted him of her arrival. He had the appearance of casual relaxation in jeans and a grey Henley that hugged his biceps and showed off the contours of his muscular torso, but his eyes were a dead giveaway. They focused on her with intensity, blaring the truth of his desire like a beacon in the night.

"Hi," she said softly, already panting.

He pulled her into the apartment with one arm around her waist and didn't lose any time kissing her hungrily and thoroughly. Layla flung her arms around his neck and willingly opened her mouth beneath his, sucking on his tongue and thrusting hers into his.

"I feel like I've waited forever for this," he said huskily, his voice sounding ravenous and thick. He sucked on her ear lobe and kissed her neck.

"Me too," Layla gasped, straining on her toes to better position the hard ridge pressing against her lower stomach. She'd anticipated this night with such longing that at times she felt as if the ache would never go away—as if her entire body had become a single throbbing nerve.

Rashad's hands lowered to her denim-clad bottom, and no more talking was necessary.

They both knew why she was there.

❧ 9 ❧

With their lips clinging to each other as if seared by the heat of metal, Rashad and Layla stumbled into the bedroom—dark and dominated by a king bed with navy sheets and six large pillows neatly stacked against each other. A large lamp cast a ghostly glow, pushing against the shadowy corners and offering a glimpse of heavy wood furniture in the room.

Rashad ravaged her mouth with deep, probing kisses, his tongue breaching her lips and his teeth teasing with stinging bites and nips. He traced the dips and curves of her body with knowing hands, and she, too, explored him—reacquainting herself with the beauty of his form. She shoved her hands beneath his shirt and caressed the warm skin covering his back and the taut muscles of his abdomen.

They stripped naked in what seemed like a matter of seconds. God, he was magnificent—tight muscles overlaid by smooth dark skin, with a body that looked like it had been sculpted from black onyx.

Rashad lowered her to the bed, and over two hundred pounds of hard male came down between her thighs. His hand slid below her belly, and he let out a satisfied groan when he found her dripping wet with want. She arched her back and eased her legs wider, her breath stuttering over her tongue as she struggled to breathe.

He savored her, lingering at the sensitive spot behind her ear before leisurely kissing her shoulders and collarbone, leaving her skin flaming in the wake of his lips. Moving lower to the tops of her breasts, he sucked and licked and squeezed his tongue into her cleavage. Layla bit down on her bottom lip, tossing her head from side to side as she ached for him to make the final foray to her painfully tight nipples.

"*Please*," she whispered, running her fingers over his soft, coily hair. That's all she could manage, unable to bear the torture any longer.

With excruciating slowness, Rashad cupped one breast and then finally—finally!—pulled her caramel nipple into his hot mouth. Layla gasped and sank her fingers into his shoulders, the overwhelming pleasure making her feel as if she were about to go mad. His teeth tugged while his tongue soothed with a velvet caress. Warm pleasure coursed through her veins and her sexual need for him surged and swelled like a rising tide.

He kissed a path down her body, hands staying busy, clearly on a mission to reclaim every inch of her. His fingers brushed her hip bone and feathered over her thighs. Her calves and ankles didn't go untouched, nor did her bottom or the curve at the base of her back when he flipped her onto her stomach.

When he swept aside her hair so his lips could touch her nape, she sighed audibly and curled her fingers into the sheets. He knew his way around a woman's body—specifically *her* body— and had turned her into a writhing mess, the interior of her thighs throbbing and sticky and wet. He buried his face in her neck, rubbing his hard dick against the crack of her ass, and she rotated her hips against him, listening with satisfaction as he gasped at her lewd movements. Arching her spine, she pushed back harder, and he shoved his fingers into her hair and tugged back her head.

He kissed her hard, hungrily, as if this might be the last time he had a chance to taste her mouth. Their lips and tongues moved over each other in a sloppy kiss that reinforced their passion and uncontrollable need for each other.

When the kiss ended, Rashad pulled Layla on top of him, and she experienced the full length of his body spread out beneath hers. She slid her hand between his legs and held his solid length in a snug clasp, stroking slowly at first and then increasing the pace, forcing him to let loose a growl of approval. His breathing grew choppy, so she knew he enjoyed her touch. When she swiped her tongue across the tip of his length, his body jerked and he grabbed her by the neck, forcing her gaze to meet his.

"Get on top of me," he demanded.

She followed his instructions and flung one leg over his hips. She sank down on top of him, gasping as she was stretched by his girth and impaled by his length. They both stilled, absorbing the moment—reveling in the sensation of being locked together. His nostrils flared and his dark eyes narrowed to slits. Rashad placed both hands on her hips and then began to move, undulating his long body in a sexy wave of movement that made her respond in kind.

Layla forgot everything that came before this moment—the doubts she had about Rashad, the uncertainty and pain of the past that forced her to make a clean break. All of that disappeared as she rode him. She moaned as his pace quickened and listened to the corresponding tufts of air that discharged from his lungs. Her breasts jostled as she bounced up and down on his shaft and fiery need built and coalesced into a perfect storm of desire.

The tender muscles between her thighs quivered around his length, and a very noticeable tightening in her lower abdomen signaled a pending orgasm. With only a few more thrusts from his hips, she'd be coming. She was so turned on by his scent and touch that she leaned forward and kissed his mouth, sucking on his plump lower lip as her hips made erotic circles, and she continued to ride him.

Rashad pumped up into her, each stroke deep and powerful. She let him take control, her hands braced on either side of his head, her weak elbows wobbling in a valiant attempt to maintain her position because she didn't want to lose one iota of this feeling of complete and blissful delirium.

"That's my girl," Rashad said, one hand roughly squeezing her ass while the other remained in place on her back. "You feel so good. He missed you, sweetness."

He being his dick. Heaven forbid that he tell her again that he—Rashad—had missed her. That moment on her street was long gone, but she wouldn't let that spoil *this* moment and take away the orgasm that was tantalizingly close.

Sitting upright, Layla cupped her breasts and tweaked her nipples to heighten the pleasure. "I'm almost there," she whispered brokenly.

"Go ahead, sweetness. Use me however you like," he grunted, the muscles in his neck corded tight as he fought to hold back and make sure she came first.

That did it.

She came unglued, falling apart at the seams, giving herself over to an orgasm that constricted her loins and made her body feel like one large nerve ending.

Rashad's hips moved faster, and Layla tossed back her head and closed her eyes to sink deeper into oblivion. The hand on her bottom moved to her left breast and Rashad alternated between squeezing the fullness of her flesh and tweaking a tight nipple between his fingertips.

She came again, hips working overtime as her body convulsed around him, loud moans spilling from her lips over and over again like a sorcerer's incantation. Rashad pulled her down and captured her cries with hungry kisses, a hand at her waist holding her in place as he continued to thrust, pulling out yet another orgasm that depleted her energy and spun the room.

When she felt she had nothing else to give and her body was drained of the ability to move, he rolled her onto her back and continued to drive into her. Now he was on top, and his knees splayed her legs wide, the full weight of his body pressing her into the soft mattress with a flurry of thrusts. His stamina was unbelievable, but so was her body's ability to respond to his. He was so damn good and multi-tasked like a boss, kissing and sucking sensitive spots on her skin while knowing the right angle to slice into her body so that he hit her G-spot over and over.

"Three years. Three goddamn years you been right here," he growled in her ear. "How dare you keep this from me."

She had no defense against such masterful lovemaking. Lifting her whole body into each thrust, she hooked her arms around his neck as he buried his face between her jaw and collarbone. The coil of tension in her loins snapped like a weakened rubber band, and she succumbed to another orgasm. At the same time his hips accelerated, her vaginal walls clenched around him and Rashad let out a hoarse, wounded sound that seemed to be torn from somewhere deep inside him.

He followed with a stream of F-bombs through gritted teeth and slammed his fist into the bed.

Their lower bodies crashed into each other over and over to unleash the full power of the climax, their muted cries mingling together in a chorus of raw, unadulterated pleasure.

❧ 10 ❧

Rashad exited the bathroom into the bedroom. Noting Layla's still body under the navy-blue sheets, he smiled to himself. No doubt, he'd put her ass to sleep. She always wanted to sleep after they made love.

So much for your no-spending-the-night rule, he thought with a silent chuckle.

He slipped under the cool top sheet and carefully placed an arm across her waist. A beat later she stiffened and eased away.

So, she wasn't asleep.

Layla sat up on the mattress and threaded her fingers though her rumpled tresses. Rashad caught his breath, eyes glued to her. All her lipstick was gone, leaving only bare lips, slightly swollen from his amorous kisses, and her hair tumbled around her shoulders in a halo of midnight strands against her tawny-gold skin. Damn, she was gorgeous.

She tucked the sheet under her arms to protect her breasts from exposure. "It's late," she said, covering a yawn with one hand.

Rashad reclined with his arms folded behind his head. "Yeah, it is."

Layla flung her legs over the side of the bed and stood. At

first he thought she might be headed to the bathroom, but then she picked up her jeans from the floor.

He lifted onto his elbows. "What are you doing?"

"Getting dressed. I'm going home," she said in a matter-of-fact voice.

He sat all the way up. "You're leaving *now*?"

"Yep." Her flippant tone landed like a slap in the face, and when she went into the bathroom with her purse and the rest of her clothes bundled in her arms, his eyes followed her in disbelief.

What the hell?

Layla couldn't seriously be planning to leave his bed in the middle of the goddamn night. Granted she'd said no spending the night at each other's place, but come on. When they first dated, he'd fallen asleep and woken up plenty of times with her in his arms. Leaving at—he glanced at the clock—almost midnight was ridiculous.

Rashad swung his legs over the side of the bed and waited for her to exit the bathroom. Minutes later, she came out fully dressed, hair brushed into a polished ponytail and her lipstick freshened.

"Listen, I know we had an agreement we wouldn't spend the night at each other's place," he began, "but you don't have to rush out. Relax. You hungry? I could make us something to eat or order in."

"It's late, and I ate earlier. Thank you for tonight, though. The sex was amazing. Exactly as I remembered."

A soft, almost benevolent smile touched the corners of her mouth and irritated the hell out of him. She was treating him like a charity case. Layla walked over and pecked him on the mouth, but his lips firmed, refusing to yield to hers.

She stepped back, a frown of surprise marring her forehead. "Something wrong?"

Yes! She rolled out of his bed in the middle of the night after 'amazing' sex. Everything was wrong.

"Nothing's wrong. Let me grab my robe, and I'll walk you out," Rashad muttered, standing.

He didn't have a stitch of clothing on, and she bit her bottom lip, her admiring gaze crawling down his naked body. "I'm so tempted to slide back into bed with you and go another round, but I better get out of here if I plan to get up at a decent hour in the morning." She lifted her Chanel purse onto her shoulder. "No need to walk me out. Call when you want to hook up again. Bye!"

She waved and stepped across the carpet in sky high stilettoes, hips swinging, stride confident—and dare he say it—a bounce in her step.

Rashad stared at the now empty doorway. Disoriented. Speechless.

Layla was in a helluva good mood, and considering he just had mind-blowing sex with her, he should be too. Instead, he was grumpy. Cranky. Annoyed. He rubbed his brow to ward off a headache and climbed back into bed.

With his back against the padded headboard, he sat in the dimly lit room and pondered what had occurred between them minutes before, unable to adequately define the odd sensation in his chest. All he knew was that having her rush out so soon after they made love left a bitter taste in his mouth. Layla had treated him as if he were simply an object for her sexual gratification. A dick to ride when she was horny, but she didn't need him for anything else.

He picked up his phone from the bedside table. Layla used to send him videos all the time. Sometimes to simply check in and say hello. Other times to update him on her day's activities. He had dozens of videos, which could be as simple as thirty seconds of her excited whispers about a delicious meal, to asking his opinion about new makeup she was trying from her friend, Tamika, who owned TamCam Cosmetics.

One of his favorites was a video of her wearing a white

bandeau top and beige wide-legged linen pants. He clicked on the image.

"Hey, baby," Layla said in the video. "I know you're busy, so that's why I didn't call. Hopefully, you'll get a chance to see this and give me your opinion. I bought this outfit for the weekend in Miami with my sisters. What do you think?" She wrinkled her nose. "I like it, but I'm not sure." She and her sisters were going to Miami to celebrate her older sister's birthday and take advantage of a weekend she had without her husband and kids.

Holding up the phone, she twisted and turned so he'd get a good look at the outfit. Smoothing a hand over her hip, she continued to talk, pointing out what she liked and didn't like, but he hadn't seen anything he didn't like and told her as much when he sent a text back. He pointed out how the top hugged and lifted her breasts and the crop top showed off her flat belly. The wide-legged pants were just right. Overall, she looked sexy without looking like she was trying too hard.

He set aside the phone and stared across at the closed bedroom door. What had happened to that Layla? The sweet, fun-loving woman he'd adored. The sex was still good, but she'd changed, and he couldn't recall ever feeling dirty after sex. Not once, and certainly never with her.

Sex with Layla had always been euphoric, emotional, and tension-relieving. Tonight was different. For the first time, he felt as if his skin and the very core of his being was covered in grime.

Sliding lower in the bed, Rashad tugged the covers up to his chin.

He'd never felt so... used.

A WIDE GRIN ON HER FACE, LAYLA PRESSED HARDER ON THE Cadillac's accelerator as she drove away from Rashad's building.

Wow. She'd actually done it. She'd had sex with Rashad and left.

Gripping the steering wheel, she let out an exultant laugh.

Granted, affecting a disinterested voice as she dressed had been difficult because the temptation to remain in his bed was very real. She'd suffered a moment of weakness while he was in the bathroom. Lying in the dark, she'd been completely lethargic and unable to move. That always happened whenever they had sex.

Under the covers, with a soft pillow cushioning her head, sleep had dragged down her eyelids, and she was fairly certain she'd dozed off for at least a few minutes. When he put his arm around her waist to cuddle, she'd wished she could stay like that forever.

Seconds later, alarm bells went off and common sense returned, but pulling out of his arms had been extremely difficult. That's why she'd moved so slowly, taking her time more out of reluctance than politeness. But getting dressed and splashing water on her face had rejuvenated her.

She could definitely get accustomed to a sex-only relationship. Though she didn't admit her reservations to her friends, she'd privately had doubts. Tonight proved those doubts were ill-placed, and simply hooking up with Rashad was doable. She was already looking forward to the next time.

Great sex without the heartache. What more could a woman want?

🎔 11 🎔

Rashad had made up his mind that he and Layla needed to talk about where this relationship was headed. Since she came over five nights ago, he'd had plenty of time to think, and there needed to be an adjustment to their no-strings affair.

Tonight, he was going to show her that they were not simply sexually compatible, but compatible, period. Before he had opened his big mouth and told her he wanted to slow down, they used to have fun together, laugh together. They'd attended comedy shows and gone to basketball games and nice dinners. Then of course there were the conversations about everything under the sun that sometimes lasted well into the night before exhaustion tugged them to sleep. Back then, they had good-natured arguments about a variety of topics—from business to politics to the latest pop culture gossip.

Time to remind her of what they used to have.

When the doorbell rang, he immediately checked his appearance in the mirror, smoothing a hand down his face and grinning. He looked great in a long-sleeved black and gold leaf shirt with black slacks. The diamonds in his ears flashed against his skin, and after a last-minute shave, a splash of aftershave made him smell good.

Rashad swung open the door. "Hi," he said.

"Hi." Layla rushed in, tugging off moleskin gloves that matched her taupe-colored coat. "Sorry, I'm late. I had a last-minute emergency to take care of."

"No worries. I just stepped out of the shower a few minutes ago."

"Good, then I'm right on time."

"Care for anything to drink?"

Rashad took her coat and hung it in the closet near the door. Underneath, Layla wore skinny jeans and a Big-Bird-yellow long-sleeved blouse with a low-dipping neckline. Exquisite, as always.

"I'm fine. Honestly, I don't have a lot of time. Only about thirty minutes, so we'll have to hurry. I have to be in Ethan's home office by nine for a Zoom meeting. He's still overseas and needs me to pull some files that he needs."

She moved quickly toward the bedroom, and Rashad followed. He watched her kick off her heels and lift her blouse over her head, placing it carefully on the chair across from the bed. For a moment he became distracted by the way the black satin bra pushed her breasts high and together, creating a tempting cleavage. But sanity returned, and he became more annoyed than aroused, perturbed by her nonchalant attitude.

"What are you doing?" Rashad asked.

Layla's hand stalled on the snap on her jeans. "What do you mean what am I doing?"

"You know what I mean."

A frown wrinkled the space between her eyes. "No, I don't."

"What the hell, Layla. Why are you treating me like a damn ho?"

Her eyes widened. "I'm not. I thought you called me over here to—"

"Yes, I called you over here to have sex, but that's not the only reason. I thought we could spend time together. Do something other than have sex."

He didn't think it was possible, but her eyes went wider, and she took a step back.

"That's not what we agreed to."

"Well, I'm changing the parameters of this arrangement. Put your blouse back on."

"Are you serious right now?"

"Yes, I'm serious. Get dressed."

Hands on her hips, she placed a gentle arch in her back so her breasts stuck out more. "Are you sure?"

Rashad's mouth went dry. No, he wasn't. In fact, he was downright struggling because he'd been reacquainted with her soft skin, sexy curves, and that tight, wet spot at the juncture of her hips. Heaven. Nirvana. Hunger ravaged his body, and he valiantly fought the urge to shove control to the side and press his face into her tempting breasts. But he'd made a promise to himself and intended to keep it, dammit.

"Yes, I'm sure." He fisted his hands, fingers pressing into his palms.

"I don't have time to go to dinner or whatever you have planned. We have to do this now or forget it."

He gritted his teeth but spoke calmly. "Then let's forget it and get together tomorrow night or later this week."

"I might have other plans. How do you know if I even have time to do that?"

He moved closer. Big mistake. The alluring scent of her perfume filled his nostrils and made the struggle to keep from touching her even harder. "*Make time*, Layla."

She glared up at him. "What game are you playing, Rashad?"

"This isn't a game. I want to spend time with you doing something other than fucking. Is that so crazy?"

Several beats passed as she eyed him with narrowed eyes. Then she flung her hands in the air in exasperation. "I don't get it. I thought this was what you wanted."

"I did, but after the last time you were here..." He shook his head, upset about the memory of how she'd screwed him and left. "I didn't like your behavior, okay?"

"My behavior? You're something else."

"I want to start over with you. I want to go to movies and dinner and do all the things we used to do together."

"Sounds too much like a relationship, which is exactly where we were years ago, which didn't work out because you wanted something different and pulled back." She pulled the yellow blouse over her head and plopped onto the mattress to put on her shoes.

Rashad snatched them up before she did, and they stared at each other, at a sort of standoff. A battle of wills.

He crouched before her and cradled one foot in his hand. She went still, and he knew she was holding her breath.

He carefully and gently placed the pump on her foot. He did the exact same to the other foot and then slid his hand up her left calf. "You think it's easy for me to let you walk out of here? It's hard as hell. Two seconds ago you were half naked. But I want more, Layla."

He gently massaged her soft flesh, and she inhaled sharply, the sound dropping like a grenade in the silence of the room. Finally, he settled on his knees, rested his arms on either side of her hips, and pushed himself between her thighs.

"I'm different," he said.

"Different how?"

"I don't want to screw around like I used to."

"Then you've changed quite a bit."

"I could say the same about you," he said.

She laughed briefly but gave no other response.

"What are you thinking?" Rashad asked.

"Trying to figure out why I should believe you when at Eli's Restaurant you quickly agreed to my suggestion that we only have sex. That makes me think not much has changed, that you want to keep me at a distance. We both know the reason you

DELANEY DIAMOND

wanted to slow down was because I was getting too close to you."

He lowered his gaze.

"You can't even look at me because I'm right," she said softly.

There were things about his past that very few people knew. They were shocking and tragic, and if she knew about the monster in his past, she wouldn't feel the same way. Though part of him wanted to share that aspect of his background with her, he worried about the fallout and doubted she could handle his secrets.

He met her gaze. "I understand you have doubts, but I'm not the same person. I'll be different. You'll see."

"I saw you, you know. After you gave me your talk, I saw you walking down the sidewalk in your neighborhood, with your arm around a woman. Blonde, pretty, and you came into your building together. When I called and asked what you were doing —to test you—you said you were out with Alex. You lied to me, because you didn't want me to know you were with another woman." Pain shimmered in her eyes.

"Blonde...?" Rashad briefly closed his eyes and groaned internally. "I know who you're talking about. That was my sister."

"She was white, Rashad."

"She's like a sister. Heather. She spent the night—"

Layla turned away, crossing her arms over her chest.

"Nothing happened because we're like family. Like Alex. She was visiting from out of town and spent the night at my place because she had an early tour leaving the next morning. My condo was more convenient than staying at Alex's. You can ask him about her if you don't believe me."

"I never heard you talk about her."

"There are a lot of things I didn't share with you."

"No kidding." She swallowed.

"That's why you called and broke up with me."

She looked him in the eyes, hers filled with hurt and sorrow.

68

He touched her cheek. "Sweetness, I swear, Heather was practically family. She died year before last."

Layla gasped. "What? Rashad, I'm so sorry."

He forced himself to go numb so he couldn't feel the pain anymore. He, Heather, and Alex had been as close as siblings, and her death had landed a devastating blow to their little family.

"She was sick for a while, and now she's in a better place. No more pain," he said, woodenly. "When you told me we were done, I was shocked. Then you refused to see me, even when I showed up at your apartment."

"I didn't want to hear anything you had to say."

"That was clear." Rashad took her hand. "Give me another shot. Let's see where we can take this. I'm all in."

Layla sighed. "I don't want to make a hasty decision. Let me think about it."

"Okay. When do you think I can see you again? Maybe Friday?"

"I'm busy. I'll call you when I'm free."

"All right. We'll do this at your pace." Rashad didn't like that answer, but he'd have to be satisfied. He couldn't push too hard because then he'd push her away.

As he helped her to her feet, her phone beeped. She pulled it from her purse and almost immediately, a smile spread on her face.

"Good news?" Rashad asked.

"Yes. I..." She hesitated.

"If it's good news, tell me."

"The text is from my sister. My dad did really well in physical therapy today. The doctor thinks he'll be able to walk without his cane soon."

"What happened to your dad?"

She responded to the text and then tucked the phone in the bag over her shoulder. "He had an accident. A guy was texting and not paying attention and side-swiped my dad's car. Banged him up pretty good. Anyway, he's been in therapy for three weeks, and there has been a lot of progress. She wanted me to know that he did well today."

"I asked about your family the other day. Why didn't you tell me about your dad?"

"Why would I?"

"It's me, Rashad," he said, suddenly angry and hurt that he'd been excluded.

He used to love hearing stories about her family, and every so often she'd FaceTime with her parents, which was always like a hilarious episode from a sitcom. He'd assumed that since both her parents were high-powered attorneys, they were staid, serious people. Instead, they were a funny, affectionate couple whose teasing and bantering made clear the decades of love between them. Each FaceTime session—and Rashad had been fortunate enough to be nearby during at least five—had been an experience.

He'd come to feel as if he knew her family, and he and Layla's mother had even exchanged cookie recipes once. Being that he didn't have a family of his own, he'd devoured each story Layla shared and enjoyed every conversation he'd had with her parents.

"We don't have that type of relationship anymore," Layla said quietly.

Her answer decimated him, and emotion clogged his airway. "We used to."

"You didn't want that, remember?" She looked at him with a doleful expression, eyes revealing the weight of the pain he must have caused. Now he understand what it felt like when someone you cared about cut you out of part of their life, and he didn't like it.

Damn, he wished he could take back that time. Knowing he'd hurt her tormented his conscience.

"I cared about you, and by default I cared about your family and your friends. Anything that matters to you matters to me,"

Rashad said. "Will you at least tell him that I'm rooting for him?"

Layla nodded. "Sure."

They walked to the front of the apartment, and he helped her put on her coat.

Rashad kissed her cheek, his arms wound loosely around her waist. "Keep me posted on your dad."

"I will."

"Look at me, Layla."

She lifted her gaze from his chest.

"I'm not going to screw this up."

"I guess we'll see how you do. Good night, Rashad."

After she left, he went to look out the window, hands stuffed into his pockets. No doubt he'd been selfish before, but losing Layla had taught him a valuable lesson. How much she meant to him. If she gave him another chance, he'd show her that he could be a different man.

The kind of man she deserved.

❧ 12 ❧

Layla stepped into Avery's Juke Joint on Peachtree Street and cast her gaze around the crowded space. She'd been to the lively spot before, where on weekends a band played funk and blues while guests created a makeshift dance floor in front of the stage. The building used to be a retail store and had been converted into an establishment that served delicious Southern cuisine and strong drinks for an eclectic crowd of professionals.

She felt great after a pampering session at the spa earlier, and she'd misted her face with a rosewater spray Tamika had recently launched. The floral scent was enough to put her in good spirits, but the product had hydrating qualities she'd come to depend on during the skin-drying winter months.

She had a date tonight and having been burned before, sincerely hoped that he looked the same as he did in the photos. She'd matched online with Garrison, who coined himself a world traveler, a good listener, and a great conversationalist. Though she had to question the last part since he'd chosen to meet her here. The loud music wasn't exactly conducive to conversation and getting to know each other.

Finally she saw him at the bar, a stark white structure that wound in an S-shape along one wall and was crowded with laughing customers who sipped cocktails and in general looked like they were having a great time. Garrison waved to get her attention, and she went over to him.

"You made it," he said, a wide grin on his face.

They hugged briefly.

He looked almost exactly like his photos. Moderately handsome with dark eyes and skin the color of brown leather. A few gray hairs were sprinkled throughout his low-cut hair, something she hadn't noticed in the images online.

"I made it."

They both laughed, and some of her nervousness disappeared.

"I was about to get a drink in case you were late or didn't show."

"You thought I might stand you up?"

"Hey, it's happened before. Online dating isn't all fun and games."

"True." She'd run into a few clods herself, though none had stood her up. They usually ended up being rude, didn't look like their photos, or were only interested in hooking up. To weed out the players, she'd been clear on her profile that she was searching for a serious relationship, but either these men couldn't read or they didn't care.

"This way. The owner is a friend of mine, and I was able to get us a table in the back."

They bypassed the crowd and went behind a wall that led to a hallway.

"I didn't realize all this was back here."

"It's a pretty big place," Garrison said.

The back room was quieter and contained five round tables, three already occupied. She and Garrison sat down at a table against the wall. A server came over immediately and took their drink and food orders and then left them alone.

Garrison clasped his hands on the table. "It's nice to finally meet you in person, and you look exactly like your photos."

Layla laughed. "I was thinking the same thing about you."

He chuckled, and then they drifted into an easy conversation that she enjoyed, but she continuously thought about Rashad and how they used to talk for hours on end about everything and nothing. She missed those conversations.

When he'd suggested seeing her tonight, she'd been sorely tempted to cancel with Garrison but reminded herself that she was within her rights to date other people. She should ignore the misplaced guilt that ate at her conscience. She wasn't doing anything wrong, and Rashad was probably doing the same.

Twirling fettuccine on her fork, she wondered, *Has he made plans with someone else?*

Pain pierced her chest, and she lifted her wine glass to her lips, giving Garrison a faint smile as he laughed for reasons she had no clue about.

She shouldn't care what Rashad was doing tonight or who he was doing it with. As long as he wasn't having sex with them, he could do whatever he wanted. Another slice of pain, sharper this time, cut into her chest and belly.

Layla shook her head and refocused on the man before her. She was looking for a husband, and he might be sitting in front of her, so she at least owed him the courtesy of paying attention.

For the rest of the night, the conversation with Garrison flowed easily, but as they neared the end of the meal, Layla accepted that there wasn't a spark. He was a nice guy, but the excitement she'd hoped for didn't exist between them.

"You seem to be in deep thought over there," he said with a mild smile.

"Do I?" Layla cracked the crust on her crème brûlée and spooned the sweet custard into her mouth.

Garrison sat back, a rueful twist to his lips. "Let me guess. You're thinking that we don't have much chemistry, am I right?"

Her eyes widened.

He chuckled. "Don't feel bad, I was actually thinking the same thing." He frowned as he searched for the right words. "I like you, but maybe we're better off as friends. Don't get me wrong, you're a beautiful woman, but... I don't feel anything, and I think I know why."

"Why?"

"Tonight was a trial run for me," he admitted. "I've been divorced for over a year and wanted to see if I was ready to get back into the game, but I'm not sure that I am."

"I'm sorry." Layla remembered from his profile that he was divorced, but they hadn't talked about his marriage or ex-wife the entire meal. She'd assumed the divorce had taken place a long time ago.

"Me too. I'm starting to think that those feelings I thought were gone forever haven't really gone anywhere at all."

His words landed like truth bombs. "You shouldn't jump back into a relationship if you're not ready. That's something I should tell myself too."

"What's your story?"

"Let's just say that I ended a relationship a few years ago, and even though I've had men in my life since then, nothing quite seems..."

"The same," he finished for her.

"Yeah." Her last conversation with Rashad didn't help. She was more confused than ever about her feelings for him. She'd thought she was over him, but having him offer her a real relationship had caused excitement and longing she'd thought had long been displaced.

"Friends?" Garrison said.

"I would like that."

He leaned forward on folded arms. "How about we finish up here and head out to the main room and do some dancing. I'm not the best dancer in the world, but I promise you'll have fun."

"I would like that," Layla said.

They finished their desserts, and Garrison paid for the meals.

Layla looped her arm through his as they made their way out of the small dining room and into the main part of the restaurant. They were winding their way past the bar when Rashad stepped in front of them, and Layla pulled up short.

Her mouth fell open in shock. "Hey, what are you doing here?"

"I could ask you the same thing." With a hard glint in his eyes, his gaze landed on their locked arms.

Layla guiltily released Garrison. "I had dinner with a friend," she explained.

"A friend?" Rashad arched a doubtful eyebrow. "Your friend is the reason you couldn't see me tonight?"

"Maybe now isn't a good time to discuss this."

"No, let's talk about this right here, right now. No better time than the present."

"Hey, buddy, calm down," Garrison said.

"I'm not your buddy," Rashad said, getting louder and jabbing a finger at Garrison.

Layla rested a hand on Rashad's arm. "Can we go somewhere and talk?"

"You sure your boyfriend won't mind?"

"He's not my boyfriend. I told you, he's a friend. I'll meet you outside in a few minutes."

Rashad glowered at Garrison before responding. "You have five minutes," he said to Layla. He stalked away into the crowd toward the door, and Layla turned to face Garrison.

"Are you sure you're going to be okay with that guy?" he asked, deep concern etched in his eyes and voice.

"He's harmless. Thanks for dinner, but, as you can see, I need to talk to him."

Suddenly, understanding dawned in his eyes. "Is he the one you were talking about? The one you still have feelings for?"

"He's the one," Layla said with a nod.

"Good luck to you." The compassion in his voice warmed her heart.

"Good luck to you, too, and please, keep in touch."

"I will. Since you're leaving, I'm going to hang out at the bar and maybe see if I can entice some other woman to dance with me."

Layla gave him a quick goodbye hug. "Take care."

❧ 13 ❧

Layla found Rashad pacing the sidewalk, an intimidating image in all black—black turtleneck, black jeans, and a black leather jacket, with a thick gold chain around his neck.

He stopped when he saw her. "What was that about? And don't tell me you weren't on a date, because I know a date when I see one. When I walked up, you were practically hanging all over him."

"I was not! For your information, we decided we were better off as friends. Yes, I was on a date, but—"

"So that's it? You get to screw around while I'm at home doing nothing?"

"Didn't look like you were sitting at home to me. Did *you* have a date?"

"No, I didn't have a date. I needed to get out of the house because I couldn't stop thinking about you, and by the way, we never said it was okay to see other people."

"That's not true. I made it very clear that I still want to find the kind of man I can have a future with. Maybe you didn't hear that, but I'm still looking. Having sex with you doesn't mean I stopped looking."

"You're still looking?" He stared at her, aghast.

"I told you that from the beginning. Why are you acting as if this is new information?"

"Because I can't believe you were serious. So I'm a filler?"

"I didn't say that."

"But that's what I am, right? Until you find the man of your dreams, you're passing the time with Rashad, riding his dick until the perfect dick comes along."

"You're making me sound like a horrible person."

"That's because you are!" he exclaimed. "What kind of sick shit is this? I'm not some seat filler, Layla. I'm a person, with feelings, in case you didn't notice."

"You jumped at the chance for a casual relationship, and now you want to act all morally righteous. You're upset because you saw me with someone else, but that shouldn't matter. We agreed that we wouldn't sleep with anyone else, but it's perfectly fine for us to keep dating until we find the right person. How can we find the right person if we don't go out with other people?"

"Are you kidding me right now?" A burst of bitter laughter fell from his lips.

"No, Rashad, I'm not. I wasn't taking myself completely off the market just to have sex with you."

Mouth hanging open, he looked genuinely surprised. "This is some bullshit."

"You got that right." She crossed her arms and looked away from him.

"Okay, you got me back, but this ends now. Tonight."

"What happened to 'We'll do this at your pace?'"

"I didn't know you were going to be seeing other men!" he yelled.

She laughed softly. "You are a narcissist. You're used to women throwing themselves at you, and the one time a woman doesn't, you lose it. You can't stand the thought that I'm not sitting by the phone waiting for your call. Guess what, I made up my mind, and I do not accept your counteroffer."

DELANEY DIAMOND

"Why not?"

"Because I said so. If you want to be with me, then we stick to the original rules. That's the only way this will work."

"And you won't consider anything else?"

"No."

"You're being unreasonable."

"And you're being unrealistic. You want me to forget what happened between us before, and I can't!"

"So you're punishing me?"

"No. I learned my lesson with you."

"Cut the crap! Do you want me or not? Tell me right here, right now." He jabbed his finger downward, at the sidewalk.

"How dare you give me an ultimatum. How do I know you're not going to change your mind again?"

"Because I'm not. Because you have to trust me, trust what we feel for each other. Because I know you feel it too. I *know*, Layla." He cupped her face. "I hurt you, and I regret it. I wish I could take it all back. The stupid conversation, the fact that you saw me and Heather without any context. The fact that I didn't call when I was aching to call, but I was too chicken to pick up the phone because I didn't think I deserved a woman like you."

Her throat clogged with tears, and her resolve weakened. He sounded so passionate and looked so sincere.

"I want to change the rules again, make you another counter-offer," he said. "No sex. We only spend time together, the way you planned to spend time with other men."

She let out a surprised laugh. "Are you capable of doing that?"

He shrugged carelessly and smiled. "I'll die trying." A pained smile crossed his face. "Not being able to slide into your tempting body will be hard, but I'm determined to prove to you that I'm not the same man. I'm not a player out solely for a good time, only interested in how many notches I can get on my bedpost. You're important to me, and I don't want to lose you again."

80

The tightness in her throat turned into a full-on lump. "No sex at all?" Layla said.

"That's right."

"Okay," she said with an air of skepticism.

"You're in?"

"I guess."

"A little more enthusiasm would be appreciated," Rashad said.

She smiled weakly. "I'm not 100 percent certain I'm making the right decision, but I'm willing to try."

"I'll take that."

He slipped his arms around her waist and pulled her flush against his body. Pressing her back against the building, he said, "Let's go on a picnic."

With his warm body nestled against hers, she could hardly think. "A picnic?"

"Yes. My building has a rooftop deck now. They added a fire pit within the past year, so it's really nice. Let's have a picnic up there. What do you say?"

She still hesitated.

"Come on, Layla. We used to have fun together all the time."

True. They had packed in a lot of activities during the six months they were together. For six months she'd been the center of his universe, drowning in his attention. Another reason why his desire to change the terms of their relationship had hurt so much.

"Yeah, we did," Layla said, a twinge of pain sprouting in her chest.

"I want to spend time with you. I know what I said three years ago, but my opinion is different. I'm different. Let me show you."

She closed her eyes. "I can't believe I'm doing this," she muttered.

"Is that a yes?"

She sighed. "Yes."

Rashad swept her up off the sidewalk and she squealed, flinging her arms around his neck.

"I'll plan everything. All you need to do is show up."

❧ 14 ❧

Rashad opened the door, and Layla gazed in at him. "Hi."

His lips spread into a pleased smile. "You showed up."

"I said I would."

"Come on in. I'm almost finished putting the food in the basket."

Because the temperature was still rather chilly, Layla dressed carefully for the rooftop picnic at Rashad's place. She pulled her long hair into a ball on top of her head and wrapped a chocolate and cream-colored cashmere scarf around her neck. The rest of her outfit included an undershirt and a cream-colored cashmere sweater, brown jeans, and high-heeled boots. Rashad was dressed warmly in layers, as well, consisting of a thin navy-blue sweater covered by a light jacket, jeans, and casual leather shoes.

When they arrived on the roof, the fire was already going strong. Flames flickered from the middle of the six foot long, concrete table and warmed the air in its immediate vicinity. Another couple sat on the long end of the cushioned L-shaped bench that faced it, and they smiled briefly and then went back to talking as Rashad and Layla went to the other end of the bench.

Rashad set the basket between them and removed the food items—hot chocolate in a flask, tomato soup, roasted chicken-and-brie grilled cheese sandwiches, and chocolate cake with chocolate icing.

"Don't tell me you made all this," Layla said.

"If I did, I'd be lying. The sandwich and soup are from the deli down the street, but I made the hot chocolate and the chocolate cake."

"Of course you made the chocolate cake," she said with a smile. She still couldn't get over that he enjoyed baking. Baking didn't seem to fit his personality at all, but he was really good at it.

"Eat up. There's plenty," Rashad said.

Layla lifted a mug of the hot chocolate to her face and paused, sniffing. "This is no regular hot chocolate. Is there alcohol in here?"

"Chocolate liqueur and vodka," Rashad answered.

Her eyes widened. "Marry me."

He chuckled. "Is that all it takes?"

"Almost." She sipped the warm drink and relished the heat as it flowed down her throat and into her chest. "Mmm, so good."

"I knew your wino ass would like that."

"Shut up! So I like a good wine and a nice drink every now and again." She cut her eyes at him and took another sip of the delicious beverage.

"What does it really take... to marry you, I mean?" Rashad asked.

Her heart raced as she wondered where he was taking the conversation. Layla glanced at him out of the corner of her eye but kept her gaze on the flickering flames. "Marriage is pretty serious. It's not something that should be entered into lightly. For me, I'd have to really know the person, inside and out."

He nodded, as if she'd said something profound. "Even when

you think you know a person, they can hide their true nature for years, though, and you'd never know."

That sounded like a loaded comment, as if he were talking about something very specific. "Being open and honest is important to building trust," Layla stated matter-of-factly.

Rashad didn't respond to that.

Her closest relationships—friendships as well as familial—were the ones where they shared the most intimate parts of each other's lives. Having someone to talk to in a nonjudgmental way created a safe space, the importance of which couldn't be underestimated. When Rashad had been less than forthcoming with information about himself and his past, the foundation of their relationship had suffered. She struggled to trust him, even as she recognized her addiction to him. When he suggested they slow down, lack of trust made it that much easier to walk away.

"What got you into baking? You have to admit, you don't look like the typical man who bakes."

He didn't answer right away, and she could tell he was about to say something important. "My foster mother used to bake bread and cakes and pies for church all the time. She and her husband were big on going to church, and they dragged me with them on Sunday and Wednesday nights."

Layla turned her entire body toward him, fully engaged and ready to soak up the tidbits he shared like a sponge. "Dragged?" she asked with amusement.

"I didn't exactly volunteer to go."

She listened with rapt attention and could see him struggling to give her more details about his background. This was the first time he'd shared this information with her, and a flutter of excitement came to life inside of her.

Usually when she inquired about his past, he clammed up or said a few vague words before moving on to another topic. He preferred conversations about the present—his life, his plans for the weekend, how he came to be the co-owner of Newmark Advisors with his best friend. Nonetheless, he was making an effort to involve her, and she relished the fact that he was pulling her closer, no matter how difficult the decision was for him.

"After a while, I didn't mind because I made friends, and there was always something going on after church—games, potluck lunches, that kind of thing."

"Did you like your foster parents?"

"Yeah, they were good people. Joe used to take me fishing, and Suzanne, his wife, would clean the fish. Depending on how much we caught, she'd have to freeze some of them, but right after one of our trips, we'd have fish for *days*—fried fish, grilled fish, whatever." He laughed softly at the memory, shaking his head. "For a thirteen-year-old kid, though, it was kinda cool to know I'd helped put food on the table. Joe also taught me a little about working on cars—how to change the oil, switch out spark plugs, that kind of thing. 'These are things every man should know how to do,' he'd say in his big voice. Man, he was loud. You could damn near hear him on the next street over." He stared down into his mug, a little smile softening the corners of his mouth.

"How long were you with them?" Layla asked quietly.

Rashad tipped the mug to his lips before he answered. "Year and a half, and then Joe got a job transfer to California. They left, and I went back into the system."

He shrugged nonchalantly, but she sensed his pain, and her heart broke at how fourteen-year-old Rashad must have suffered. Their departure had to have been difficult for him. He'd talked briefly about his family before, and she knew his parents had passed away when he was very young. That's how he ended up in foster care. He never talked about his foster parents before, but listening to his memories, and hearing that... something in his voice, let her know those people had meant the world to him.

"Did you stay in touch after they left?"

"We did at first, but then we fell off. They got busy, I got busy. It wasn't realistic to stay in touch."

"That's too bad. Were you ever placed with another family?"

"By the time Joe and Suzanne moved, I was almost fifteen, and no one wants a kid that age. When I turned sixteen, I left."

Cradling the mug of hot chocolate on her lap, Layla asked, "What do you mean you left?"

"I left. I packed up my clothes and my few possessions, and I left the home. I didn't tell anyone where I was going. I bought fake documents on the street and started at another school, rented a room in a boardinghouse, and got a part-time job."

Layla's mouth fell open. "You've been on your own since you were *sixteen*?"

"Yep."

She couldn't imagine making such a drastic move. She'd lived a sheltered, upper-middle-class life. At sixteen her biggest concerns had been going on her first date, attending junior prom and other parties, or hanging out with her girlfriends. Certainly not working, paying rent, or figuring out how to survive. At that age, she hadn't been anywhere near mature enough to go out on her own and gained new respect for Rashad.

"You never told me any of this before."

He stretched an arm across the back of the bench and smoothed the stray hairs at her nape in an upward motion. "I'm trying to do better, like I promised. You said you want me to be more open, and I'm working on it."

"I have to admit, I had my doubts."

"I know," he said with a smirk.

"You can't blame me. I used to wonder if you were in the CIA, you were so secretive."

He let out a short laugh. "Nah. Definitely not in the CIA," he said.

❦ 15 ❦

On the rooftop, with the distant sounds of cars and people so far away, they seemed to be in a different world. They ate in silence for a while. The sandwich was delicious, the cheese gooey and contrasting nicely with the seasoned chicken. Rashad had made a good choice for the meal.

Dabbing the corner of her mouth, Layla giggled to herself as the cold temperature reminded her of the funny circumstances around the first time she met Rashad.

"What?" he said, right before he placed the last morsel of his sandwich into his mouth.

"I was thinking about how we met ice skating at Atlantic Station. I was with Tamika, and you bumped into me, almost knocking me and you to the ground. Thanks to my excellent skating skills, however, I was able to keep us upright." She sat up straighter, preening and cocky.

"You think it was your excellent skating skills, huh?"

"Of course. I've been ice skating since I was six."

As a child in D.C., she and her family went ice skating every winter, even her father. He didn't actually get on the ice with them, but he went along for the family bonding time. Her older siblings used to go off on their own, doing tricks, skating backward, and in general showing off. Layla and her younger brother skated close to their mother, but as they became older, they developed the same showmanship as their older siblings.

Rashad leaned closer and dropped his voice, a spark of mischief lighting his dark eyes. "What if I told you I could skate —maybe not as well as you, but well enough? I didn't need your help that day, and we weren't going to fall when I bumped into you because I bumped into you on purpose."

Layla's mouth fell open. "What?"

"I orchestrated the whole thing. I was actually at the rink with another woman." Rashad eased back over to his side and pulled a slice of chocolate cake from the basket.

"You have got to be kidding me."

"I saw you and Tamika arrive, and I couldn't take my eyes off you. I told my date I didn't feel well, took her home, and then rushed back to the rink. Before you think the worst of me, it was our first date. I'd just started seeing her, but the minute I saw you..." He shook his head. "She didn't stand a chance. No one did."

Damn this man. He was going to make her melt in the frigid air.

"I had no clue that's what you did. I thought you were embarrassed by what happened because you bought me and Tamika season tickets to the rink."

"I had to make up for almost knocking you down."

"You said that's what dinner was for."

"Dinner was for me, an excuse to get you alone, away from Tamika. I could tell she didn't like me then, and I don't think she ever did, did she? Tell the truth."

"Umm..." Layla hedged.

"Yeah, I know," he said with a laugh.

"That's my girl. She was looking out for me, that's all."

"I get it. Same thing Alex and I do—look out for each other." Rashad ate a forkful of cake.

Layla watched him with new eyes. "I'd always felt like you

know so much about me, but I didn't know much about you. I've learned a lot today," she said quietly.

He grinned and set down his plate. "Since you're in such a good mood, this is the perfect time to ask you a question."

"Don't push your luck," Layla quipped.

"You're going to want to do this, trust me. Have you heard of Lion Mountain Vineyards in North Georgia?"

"Heard of them but never visited." The vineyards were located about an hour outside of Atlanta, in Dahlonega.

"I want to go check it out, and I want you to come with me. We'll spend the weekend, do a tour of the property, drink wine, eat good food, and then come back. Just me and you, like old times."

She bit her bottom lip and joy sprang to life in her chest. "I like that idea."

"So that's a yes?"

"Yes," Layla said softly.

Rashad took her mouth in a kiss, and she tasted the sweetness of the chocolate cake. His mouth was sensually thorough, and his tongue teased the corners of her mouth, heating her loins.

When he withdrew, Rashad licked his lips and Layla blushed at the possessive gleam in his eyes. They may not plan to have sex, but he sure wanted to, and if she were being honest, she also wanted to.

Minutes later, they were on the rooftop alone because the other couple had gone back downstairs.

"It's going to rain," Layla remarked, gazing up at the storm clouds forming in the sky.

No sooner had the words left her lips than fat drops started pelting them.

Rashad let out a mild curse. "Let's go."

They packed up the basket and turned off the fire. Then they scampered through the door and clambered down the stairs to the elevator. In Rashad's condo, Layla smoothed her edges and then took the towel Rashad handed her.

"Quite an interesting end to the afternoon," she commented, dabbing her cheeks.

"I was hoping the day wouldn't end now."

"What do you have in mind? You want to play cards or watch TV?"

"No. Those all require us to stay vertical. The activity I have in mind requires us to be horizontal."

Layla bit the corner of her lip and remained in place as he moved closer. "I thought you said no sex. You said you could handle it."

"Yeah, I did, didn't I?"

He stepped right up on her, his warm breath brushing across her lips, the heat of his body mingling with the heat from hers.

"Are you changing the rules again, Rashad?" Layla asked, breathless with anticipation.

"Are you letting me?"

"Yes." That was the only answer she could give. No point in pretending she didn't want him, because she did—almost every minute of every hour.

Rashad's lips landed on hers with a soft press before he maneuvered them toward the bedroom. Inside, they undressed each other, interrupting the removal of their clothes with soft laughter and more kissing.

They fell onto the bed, and Layla gasped as his hard flesh sank into her. She gladly welcomed him into her body, arms and legs wrapped tightly around him as they rocked back and forth.

She sucked on his lower lip and kissed his Adam's apple, the decibels of her moans increasing as his thrusts became harder.

No man had ever made her lose her mind like this. No man had ever taken such control of her body and heart. As she climaxed around him, Layla hoped that Rashad continued to share with her. She didn't just want his body. She wanted his heart and needed to know that he welcomed her into his life the same way she welcomed him into hers.

۞

NORMALLY, LAYLA WOULD GO TO SLEEP AFTER THEY MADE love, but she hadn't eaten her chocolate cake, so Rashad went to get it and they took turns eating it in bed while using the same fork.

"I shouldn't be sharing my cake with you because this slice is mine. You already ate yours," Layla said, as she opened her mouth for him to slide in another piece.

"Too late now, it's almost gone," Rashad said with zero remorse.

When they finished eating, he placed the fork and plate on the bedside table and pulled Layla back against him as he sat up against the headboard.

"That was delicious," she said.

"Of course. I made it."

"You're so modest."

He kissed the back of her head, and she played with the curly hairs sprinkled on his forearm.

"When do you want to go up to Lion Mountain Vineyards?" Layla asked.

"Next weekend work for you?"

"I'll have to check with Ethan, but it shouldn't be a problem."

Rashad grunted.

Layla threaded her fingers through his and then tilted her head sideways to look at him. That gave her a good view of the stubborn set to his jaw. "You know there's nothing going on between me and Ethan, right?"

"Maybe not, but I believe he wants you. He pays for your loft, Layla, and you didn't have that Cadillac SUV when we were dating, so I already know he bought that for you."

"He owns the building and lets me stay in the loft for free, so I basically consider that part of my salary. As for the Cadillac, he leased it for me because I have to run errands for him all the time, and he wants me to have a dependable vehicle."

"He treats everybody like that?" Rashad asked, with a skeptical lift of his right eyebrow.

"Not everybody, but the people he depends on the most. Do you know what he did for his executive assistant, Daria? She's a single mom, and he covered her son's college tuition for all four years. Daria was crying in the office, she was so grateful."

"All right, the man's a freaking saint," Rashad grumbled.

"Not a saint, but generous." Layla resettled against his chest, pulling his arms tighter around her waist. "I'm really looking forward to this weekend trip. Memorial Day weekend in Myrtle Beach was fun, remember?"

"Yeah, that was nice." Rashad chuckled. "Except for when the guy in the condo next door was hooking up with a woman who was *not* his wife."

"Oh my goodness, that's right!" Layla said.

The day before, she and Rashad had run into a couple and their two children in the hall and learned they were staying next door. They chatted for a bit before entering their individual units. The next day, after returning from the beach, she and Rashad went out onto the balcony overlooking the water, and minutes later heard what could only be described as sex noises—gasps of pleasure and feminine cries—coming from next door because the neighbor's sliding glass door was open. The problem was, she and Rashad had left the wife and kids down on the beach, which meant the husband was having sex with someone else.

"What a slime bag. Who has their mistress meet them in the same place they're having a family vacation? I wanted to tell his wife so bad. Why did you talk me out of it?"

"Because it was none of our business, and that guy looked

like the type to carry a concealed weapon. I wasn't trying to get shot for snitching."

Layla burst out laughing, and they argued some more about whether they should have gotten involved. The conversation segued into other vacation spots they wanted to visit, including taking a long cruise to Alaska, which they both longed to do.

They talked for hours, until right before midnight. As raindrops continued to pelt the window, Layla turned on her side and Rashad wrapped his arms around her and shoved a thigh between her legs. Almost immediately, his even breathing signaled he'd fallen asleep, and for her part, sleep burned her eyes. Tonight's date was a fresh start, and she welcomed the new openness between them, as well as reminiscing about the past, something she used to find difficult to do because of the all the hurt from his rejection.

Layla shifted under the covers. Rashad muttered something in his sleep, and his arms tugged her closer, holding her unusually tight.

That's how she fell asleep—snuggled in his arms, listening to the pitter patter of raindrops against the window.

❦ 16 ❦

"**A**re you ready to go? You have everything?" Rashad asked. "Because once we're on the road, I'm not turning around."

"Would you hush," Layla said with a laugh. "I'm very ready."

Excited about the weekend getaway, Layla had done research on Lion Mountain Vineyards and learned the business was not very old. A couple bought the land and started growing grapes fifteen years ago. In that short time, they'd become well known by wine lovers throughout the southeast and beyond, numerous lists naming them among the best wineries on the east coast.

Rashad took her suitcase and placed it in the back of the SUV he had rented for the one-hour trip north. He opened the door for her, and as she was about to slide in, he grabbed her butt and pulled her in for a brief kiss. She smiled up at him, her heart tightening with excitement. Optimism was the word of the day, because though she still believed her relationship with Rashad to be tenuous, this weekend together demonstrated they'd come a long way. They ate dinner together twice during the week, and one night he stayed over at her place and they binge-watched the latest Jack Ryan series on Prime Video. That was a bad idea, because it had Rashad scrambling to get to work the next morning because he'd overslept.

She slid into the passenger seat, and Rashad went around to the driver side. They pulled away from the curb and started the short journey with soft music pouring from the speakers.

They cruised along, seeing very little traffic, chatting and discussing the plans for the weekend. Rashad had scheduled them for dinner upon arrival, tomorrow they would take a tour of the property on foot and by horseback, and later in the afternoon return for a wine tasting and then dinner. Sunday they'd indulge in the property's famous brunch before taking the drive back to Atlanta in the early afternoon.

Layla's phone rang, and she looked down to see her mother was calling on FaceTime. She answered. "Hi, Mom."

"Hey, honey, what are you up to?"

JoAnn Fleming was in her newly remodeled kitchen, her hair pulled neatly back from her face, a gold necklace her husband had given her twenty-odd years ago hanging around her neck.

"I'm on my way to Lion Mountain Vineyards with Rashad."

Because she talked to her parents regularly, they already knew that she and Rashad had rekindled their relationship. They'd told her to be careful, but her parents had liked him and wouldn't be openly rude.

"Oh, that's right, that was today. Hello, Rashad."

"Hello, Mrs. Fleming."

"How are you doing?"

"Excellent," Rashad replied.

"That's good to hear. Layla, I won't keep you long. I just wanted to check in with you. Your father's here, and he was not a good patient this week. He missed two of his therapy sessions."

"I'm not surprised since he complained that he didn't want to go three times a week."

"But that's what the doctor ordered," JoAnn said.

Her father yelled from somewhere in the background. "I'm right here. Stop talking about me like I'm deaf."

"I swear, one of these days, I'm going to walk right out of this house and never come back." JoAnn rolled her eyes.

"You ain't going nowhere." Herschel took the phone and looked directly at Layla. "Where is she going after forty-two years? Huh? Ask her that. She's stuck with me. Too late now."

Her mother took back the phone. "You see what I have to put up with? Forty-two years of this." She shook her head.

"Mom, be nice, he's suffering."

"Thank you, baby," her father said.

"Don't encourage him," JoAnn said sternly, side-eyeing her husband.

"I'm a grown man, and I can do as I please, JoAnn. I been running this house all these years, haven't I?"

Rashad chuckled softly, shaking his head because he knew her father was going to pay for that remark.

"You have lost your mind if you think you run this house," JoAnn said.

"It clearly states, in the book of Herschel, chapter five and verse six, 'The man is the head of the household and shall be obeyed in all things.'"

"Dad, you're just digging that hole deeper," Layla said, hiding her laughter behind her hand.

"Are you listening to this?" JoAnn asked. "He wants me to put him back in the hospital."

"What did you say?" Herschel asked.

Layla caught a glimpse of him coming up behind her mother, and then JoAnn shrieked and the phone clattered to the counter.

"Herschel, behave!"

Laughter filled her mother's voice, countering the unintelligible words Layla's father was saying. He was probably whispering dirty words in her ear while at the same time feeling her up. Layla rolled her eyes. Her parents were so embarrassing.

Moments later, her mother's face reappeared on the screen. Smoothing her hair, JoAnn said, "I'm going to hang up now and finish fixing dinner for your father."

Herschel's face came into view over her mother's shoulder. "Dinner is what the old folks call it," he said, with a lewd grin.

"Ew. You two are gross. Goodbye," Layla said.

"You kids be safe on that road at night. Rashad, drive carefully with my little girl," Herschel said.

"Not to worry, Mr. Fleming."

"Bye, honey. Love you," JoAnn said.

"Love you," Layla returned.

She hung up with a shake of her head.

"Your parents haven't changed, I see," Rashad said with a chuckle.

"Not at all."

The minutes passed quickly on their night time drive through the mountain roads, during which Rashad placed his hand on her thigh, a casual but possessive move. He touched a lot, and being from a big affectionate family, she appreciated that part of his personality. Layla concentrated on the warmth of his hand as he talked. Little did he know that having his hand resting on her thigh was the equivalent of foreplay.

They finally arrived at the winery, a sprawling Craftsman-style building atop a hill with a huge balcony and bright lights filling the many windows. The SUV climbed the steep incline to the upper parking lot, and Layla stepped out and stretched her arms above her head before buttoning the top buttons on her burnt orange pea coat to protect against the cold mountain air.

"Let's go check in," Rashad said.

There were three floors in total, and they entered at the top, where they were greeted by the building's rustic design, high ceilings and polished wood floors. The delicious aroma of dinner and the gentle hum of conversation wafted through the doors that led into the main dining room. Once they checked in, they drove the short distance from the main building to the three-bedroom cabin Rashad had rented for them. They didn't need that much space, but Layla was immediately impressed by the interior. Decorated in warm colors, with a fireplace in the main room and French doors that opened onto a veranda that over-looked the mountains, she already imagined sitting out there in the morning, sipping coffee as she slowly woke up along with the rest of the property.

They didn't spend much time in the cabin because they were both hungry, not having eaten a single bite before they hit the road because they'd agreed to save their appetite for the expected delicious meal. A friendly hostess greeted them at the door and led them to a table in the packed dining room. Layla followed behind the young woman, glancing at the dishes along the way, her mouth watering with jealousy each time a meal caught her eye.

When they were seated, Layla leaned toward Rashad and whispered, "I think I want everything on the menu."

He chuckled, his indulgent smile warming her insides. "You can have anything you want, all weekend."

"Hmm. You're not trying to buy my affection, are you, Mr. Greene?" She batted her eyelashes at him.

Biting his bottom lip, he let his gaze travel over her loose hair and the cashmere sweater that molded to her breasts like a second skin. "I thought I already had your affection."

"You do," she admitted. "But you're trying to buy something, aren't you? So what is it?" She rested her chin on her hand and gazed across at him.

"Your l—" He paused, pulling up short. "Loyalty."

Rashad dipped his gaze to the menu, but Layla continued to watch him, a rush of heat filling her chest.

Had he been about to say *love*?

She gazed down at the choices of the prix fixe menu, heart racing with the speed of a rocket in her chest. A few years ago she wouldn't have suspected Rashad could be afflicted by the same emotion as ordinary people, but now she wasn't so sure, and her own feelings were a complicated mess. She'd loved him back then and had fully expected and wanted to be the woman who made him settle down. His lackluster responses to her talks about their future and his suggestion they slow down had put the kibosh on long-term plans. Now, however, she again saw the possibility of a future with him and recognized the intensity of her feelings hadn't disappeared. She'd hidden them in an act of self-preservation. Rashad was still the only man who could make her blush and giggle like a school girl and scream like a wanton in bed.

A weekend away made her fantasies return no matter how much she told herself she shouldn't go down that road. They were still in the probationary period, but her heart wouldn't listen. She wanted a future with him. Was it possible he was serious and wanted a future with her, as well?

They remained silent until a waitress appeared to discuss the food options and wine pairings. For the moment, Layla put aside thoughts of marriage and babies and focused on the meal. And what a meal it was.

They dined on cornmeal crusted fried oysters and mixed greens with a honey lavender vinaigrette for the salad course. For the entrée, they ate Châteaubriand, Panko-crusted scallops with parsnip purée, and roasted Brussels sprouts and butternut squash with a balsamic glaze. The meal ended with delicious chocolate hazelnut mousse tartlets topped with house made mascarpone whipped cream. The recommended wine pairings for each part of the meal were the perfect match. At the end of the dinner, all Layla could do was close her eyes and sigh contentedly.

"This has got to be one of the best meals I have ever had," she said.

The dining room was half empty now, with other guests lingering over wine and several huddled together outside on the balcony in the dark.

"I have to agree with you, that was fantastic." Rashad patted his stomach.

"I had no idea the wineries in Georgia were this good."

"This particular area has eight different wineries, and they've all won awards, including international ones. Lion Mountain has won over 200."

"The website did mention some of them," Layla said.

"They've been in direct competition with some of the California houses, and won, and *Wine Enthusiast* magazine listed them among its top ten wineries for weddings."

"Do we even need to do the tour tomorrow? You seem to know a lot about this place already," Layla said with a smile. She'd never seen him so enthusiastic about much other than investing, so she was genuinely impressed by his knowledge and obvious excitement. "How did you find out about this place specifically?"

"Alex. He and Sherry have come up here a few times, and they both enjoyed themselves. He told me I should come up here. It's a nice place for an escape, don't you think?"

"Absolutely."

"And..." Rashad dropped his voice. "We're thinking about buying it."

Layla gasped. "What?"

Rashad nodded. "You heard me. The owners want to sell because their kids aren't interested in taking over. I'm actually here to check it out, see if I agree and if we should take the leap, but they don't know. So..." He took her hand. "I need your help examining the place, if you don't mind."

She squeezed his fingers, excited for him but also delighted that he'd included her in the secret. "I'll take notes. I'll do whatever you need me to do. Baby, I'm so excited for you."

"It's not a done deal yet, but we'll see." He shrugged.

The waitress arrived, and he released her and paid for the meal.

As they strolled back to the cabin, Layla clung to him and rested her head against his arm.

Rashad remarked, "I'm glad we walked over. I need to walk off some of that food we ate."

"Me too," she admitted.

Layla shivered, and Rashad slipped an arm around her shoulders. "Cold?"

"A little chilly, but not too bad. I'm from D.C., remember?"

"Oh, right. This is like summertime for you."

They both laughed.

Inside the cabin, they made their way to the bedroom, and Layla went to stand in the bathroom doorway. She turned to face him. "I'm going to take a shower."

Kicking off his shoes, Rashad looked up. "Need some help?"

"Yes, please," she said, in a soft, girly voice.

Her heart beat faster as Rashad came closer. He was so masculine and unapologetically male.

He cupped her face and lowered his mouth to hers, nipping gently at her bottom lip and sliding his hands down her waist, over her curves, as if forming her body from clay.

They undressed slowly and stepped into the large shower stall. Layla rubbed the soapy washcloth over his skin, taking extra care to clean the turgid staff that stood upright between them. His groans encouraged her to continue, and when he took her mouth in a hungry kiss, she pressed her hard nipples into his slick skin.

Layla sucked on his lower lip and giggled against his mouth when he groaned and cursed. By the end of the shower, he had lifted her against the marble wall and took her with a rough thrust, pushing her into the hard surface, hands gripping her buttocks as his hard dick tunneled deep into her body.

Later, they stepped out of the shower and dried off and fell into bed. Layla was content, exhausted but satisfied, and looked forward to the day ahead.

❧ 17 ☙

Rashad stepped onto the cabin's balcony and filled his lungs with fresh air. Seeing the property in the daylight was an entirely different experience. The views were impressive, with rolling hills and trees as far as the eye could see.

Layla was already outside, her long, dark hair resting on the fluffy white robe, knees pulled into her chest on the lounge chair. She gazed out at the sunrise as she sipped coffee, smiling briefly at him as he pulled a chair next to her and sat down.

"I wish I could stay here forever," she said. "It's magnificent. I feel so relaxed."

"Maybe you needed a break."

"I think I did. I'm always going, going, going because of Ethan, and of course having five siblings means there's always something going on—weddings, baby showers, gossipy group chats." She sighed. "But this... this is nice. You should buy the winery for the view alone."

"Speaking of your family, your dad is a trip."

"He drives my mom and my siblings batty. If he followed the doctor's orders, he'd get better faster, but of course he has to do things his way. He's so stubborn."

"So that's where you get your stubbornness from?"

"Hey..." Layla cut her eyes at him.

Rashad laughed, but his gaze settled on her in a new way. She looked a lot like her mother—a well put together woman with the same tawny-gold skin, but her mother's dark hair was shorter and contained strands of gray. If he had to guess, he'd say Layla's personality was a combination of both her parents. She had her mother's style and engaging personality, but she also had her father's attitude when she was upset. She didn't have any problem giving Rashad a piece of her mind or cutting him off, and from what he'd heard about Mr. Fleming's courtroom style, those were his genes.

Listening to her parents last night had been nice and reminded him of the first iteration of their short-lived romance. Layla had always been generous with stories about her family, too, and he wished he also had happy, funny stories to share. His life hadn't been completely miserable, and he knew there were people who had it worse, but since he never knew his mother, and his father had been a predator of the worst kind, he preferred not to think about those days, or the days he lived alone in that little boarding house. As far as he was concerned, his life didn't begin until he turned eighteen. At college, he was reborn. A new man.

Rashad took Layla's hand. Her fingers were warm from hugging the cup of coffee. He kissed her knuckles and rested his head against the chair's back to enjoy the silence.

He wished Heather could have met Layla. He hated how she'd been taken from him and Alex, disease ravaging her body as she lay in the hospital. Life could be so unpredictable. She would've liked this place.

Though he strived to avoid pain and loss, somehow they always found him. One minute everything was fine, then the next a tragic event could suck away all the joy and leave you stranded, tossed about on a sea of emotion without a paddle. Navigating those tumultuous waters was difficult at best, soul-crushing at worst. He was very tired of soul-crushing.

That's why he'd never been able to admit that he loved Layla. That's why their relationship had been difficult and he'd tried to mitigate the damage before the universe saw fit to remove her from his life, but after last night's near slip at dinner, he couldn't deny his feelings. He loved her. More than he realized he'd been capable of loving a woman. Opening up to her still scared the hell out of him, but as he became more confident in the relationship, he suspected he'd become more courageous and share the more private parts of his life.

Maybe he could avoid pain this time. He wanted the world for Layla, and the fact that she already loved this place so much helped him make up his mind about turning the property into the next business venture for him and Alex.

He still had a lot to tell Layla, but for now he'd simply enjoy their time together.

AFTER A BIG BREAKFAST, RASHAD AND LAYLA WENT TO THE first appointment of their very full day of activities. They joined a group of ten in the cask room and cellar, where they learned how wines were made, and the guide explained about the different varietals and how the wines were stored before deemed ready for consumption. They also visited the wine library, a quiet, small space filled with artifacts that told the history of winemaking. Rashad mentally took note of all the information shared, as well as the professionalism of the woman giving the tour.

The group whittled down to six, which included two other couples, once they went out on horseback. The knowledgeable male guide explained the history of the property and about the types of grapes they grew, as well as the accolades they'd received over the years. The owners, along with staff, had planted ten thousand vines by hand, and Lion Mountain grew French grapes in the red Georgia clay, which was similar to the soil in France. The couple chose this location because of the sun exposure, which resulted in the ripest fruit possible, ensuring the highest level of sweetness and flavor.

On two occasions they climbed off the horses and experienced the property up close, walking among the vines and learning how to properly pick the grapes. Rashad took multiple pictures of Layla on horseback as well as posing among the vines. She took his breath away. He was addicted to her smiles, and the camera loved her.

When they returned to the main building, it was time for the afternoon wine tasting. They sat next to one of the couples they'd toured with earlier, tourists from out of town who happened to find out about the area through a hotel brochure.

"I think we have a new favorite place to visit on a regular basis," the woman said, smiling at her husband. She had short dark hair and bright gray eyes.

"Definitely," he agreed, in a heavy bass. He looked to be of Middle Eastern descent and much older than his wife by at least fifteen years.

"We've visited wineries in Napa, so I have to admit to being impressed by this location. Who knew Georgia had such great options."

"A hidden gem, for sure. I'll definitely be back," Layla said, talking across Rashad.

They chose six pours, and each wine had a unique and delicious flavor. At the end of the tasting, they went into the retail store and Layla picked up several bottles to take back to Atlanta for herself and her best friends.

Later, after they'd showered and were dressing for dinner, Rashad asked, "So what do you think? You think me and Alex should take the risk?"

"I absolutely love this place," Layla said, zipping up her slacks. "But what do you and Alex know about making wine? It's a lot different from what you do now."

"We can learn about wine-making, and to be honest with

you, we plan to leave everything almost exactly as is. The couple selling the place offered to stay on as managers for a year after the purchase, and they told Alex they'd be willing to act as consultants after that. Plus, we plan to keep all the staff. I've been really impressed with the employees."

Layla nodded. "Me too. Sounds like you have everything figured out. I say go for it."

"Yeah?"

"Yeah. Tamika and her fiancé are looking for a venue for their wedding, and this would be really nice, and it's not far from Atlanta. Plus, me and my girls can come here as a getaway on the weekends."

"So it's all about you and your girls?" Rashad asked, sauntering over to where she stood.

Layla laughed, wrapping her arms around his torso. "A teeny tiny bit about me and my girlfriends, but also about you. I'm excited for you. Go for it."

"Thanks, sweetness."

"I'm glad we came here. It was a nice getaway, and I... I feel like we're closer." She sounded hesitant, eyes searching his.

"We are," Rashad confirmed, kissing her soft lips.

Then he took her hand and led the way to dinner.

ON THE DRIVE BACK TO ATLANTA, THEY WERE BOTH QUIET. Brunch had been another outstanding meal with delicious offerings, and Layla already missed the winery and the escape it provided.

When Rashad pulled up outside her loft, she sighed. "Back to reality," she moaned.

Rashad turned off the engine and turned to her. "Stay the week with me."

Layla stared at him.

He took her hand. "Pack a suitcase and come stay at my place for the rest of the week... or longer, if you want."

"What prompted that offer?"

"Been thinking a lot, about you and me and how I screwed up before. I love spending time with you, Layla. This weekend was the best I've had in a long time, and I'm not ready to be apart from you. Say yes."

Emotion clogged her throat. Same as he did, she'd enjoyed the couple of days they spent together. Not only the scenery but the company. Horseback riding, teasing each other out on the balcony, and enjoying delicious food. They were of the same mind in so many ways, and she definitely wanted to spend more time with him and get to know him even better. Without a doubt, she was confident Rashad was her future.

Layla leaned over and kissed him. "Yes."

❧ 18 ❧

Layla hauled her bags from the back of the SUV. She loved a good sale and found some cute discounted pieces for spring on a spur-of-the-moment trip to the mall.

"Where are you?" she asked into the phone wedged against her ear.

"Still at the office, but I'm almost finished. I'm ironing out a few details for the Lion Mountain contract with Alex," Rashad replied.

"You had all day to do that," Layla chided him.

"Ha, ha. You're funny."

"Should I leave without you?" she asked, slamming the Cadillac's door.

"No, I'm coming. Leaving in thirty minutes."

She could hear him shuffling papers on his desk. "Hurry up. I don't want to be late for the ceremony."

Along with other teachers, Dana was being given an outstanding teacher award in a ceremony that recognized her contributions in her field, as well as her commitment to her job and fostering a welcoming environment for students that allowed them to excel. Layla and Tamika had made sure they were free tonight since Dana's family, who lived out of state, was not able to fly in for the ceremony. They had to be there to support their girl. Tamika's fiancé Anton would be there, Layla had invited Rashad, and Dana's male friend Omar would also be in attendance.

"Hurry up," she said.

"Yes, dear."

Layla smiled as she made her way to the front of his building. "I don't need the sarcasm."

"If we're late, it won't be my fault. You know how long it takes you to get ready."

"For your information, I'm already at your place, so all I have to do is jump in the shower and put on my clothes."

"And do your make up, and your eyelashes, and your hair, and—"

"Okay, okay, I get it. I'll be ready, and you need to get here so you can be ready too."

"I can leave sooner if you let me off this phone."

"Fine. Bye!"

Smiling and shaking her head, Layla hung up and entered the building. "Good evening, Liam," she said, smiling at the night-time doorman.

"Hello, Ms. Fleming. Oh, one minute, please." He held up a finger. "I have a package for Mr. Greene." He lifted a thick yellow envelope from beneath the desk and handed it to her.

During the past month, she spent so much time at Rashad's condo that she no longer needed a password to get upstairs. They allowed her to go straight up, like any one of the other owners, and per Rashad's instructions, gave her the same privileges regarding his home that he had.

"Thank you." Layla shot a cursory glance at the name written on the front. It was addressed to Deshawn Reddick. "This isn't a package for Rashad," she said, extending the envelope to Liam.

He didn't accept, nodding his head with certainty. "Yes, it is. We've received packages with that name on it before."

"Who's Deshawn Reddick?" Layla asked.

Liam shrugged.

"Okay, I'll make sure he gets it. Have a good evening." Maybe he was allowing a friend to mail packages to his address.

"You do the same, ma'am."

As the elevator climbed the building's floors, she looked at the front of the envelope, noting the Texas postmark.

"Who the heck is Deshawn?" He'd never mentioned that name before.

Layla entered the condo and tossed the envelope on a table in the living room. Then she took her bags into the bedroom and started getting ready.

When Rashad arrived, she was already dressed in a royal blue long-sleeved dress, hair swept to one side and held in place with a gold clip, but walking around barefoot in her stockings. When she heard the door open, she rushed into the living room.

"Finally, you're here. I was going to leave if you didn't show up soon. Could you zip me up?" She presented her back to him.

"How were you going to leave with your dress undone?" Rashad teased. He pulled up the zipper and then twisted her around for a kiss, which she'd grown accustomed to since spending so much time at his place. The kiss greeting had become one of her favorite acts of affection.

"I was going to ask Liam to zip me up."

"Like hell," Rashad muttered, heading toward the bedroom.

She loved teasing him, and he indulged her vanity by acting jealous every time she mentioned the possibility of another man taking his place for any reason.

"Hurry up. You have fifteen minutes to get ready," Layla said, following.

Rashad stopped. "Fifteen minutes? You know what, I'll go in what I'm wearing and shower when I get back. How long do you think we'll be out?"

"Probably for the rest of the night. After the ceremony, we're going for drinks to do a little additional celebrating."

"Oh right, I forgot. I don't want to make you late, I'll go like this."

Most days Rashad wore a suit to work, often in flashy, attention-getting colors, and today was no different. He wore a dark red suit with a black shirt and black tie. What looked tacky on other men was the perfect attire for his personality, and his dark skin was the ideal backdrop for dramatic colors.

"You look nice, so you don't have to worry about being underdressed. If you're going like that, then you're ready. I need to put on my shoes and we can leave."

Layla bypassed him to the doorway and then paused. "By the way, there's a package for you over there on the table. Liam handed it to me as I was coming up. It's addressed to someone named Deshawn."

His head swung sharply in her direction. "Did you open it?"

"No, of course not." His question surprised her. She'd never invade his privacy like that. She watched him walk over to the table and pick up the stuffed envelope. "Who's Deshawn?"

Rashad kept his gaze on the package. "I don't know," he said in such a low voice, she barely heard him.

Confused by his response, Layla padded over to where he was standing and placed a hand on his arm. Rashad started, as if she'd yanked him from a dream. "Sorry, I didn't mean to scare you. Liam said you've gotten packages for this person before, so you must know who he is."

"I don't know what Liam is talking about. It's clearly a mistake."

"I can't believe Liam would make a mistake like that," Layla said quietly.

"Well, he did," Rashad insisted.

He looked her right in the eyes, and she knew without a doubt that he was lying. Who was Deshawn Reddick, and why didn't he want her to know about him?

"Is everything okay?" she asked.

That sense of unease she used to experience with Rashad

returned—as if he was holding something back and erecting an invisible fence of privacy between them. They'd been so close recently that the feeling was particularly distressing.

"Everything is fine. I'll deal with that when I get back." He dropped the envelope on the table and took two steps away. Then he circled back and picked up the package, tucking it under his arm as he went into the kitchen.

Dumbfounded, Layla stared after him. Rashad was clearly lying to her, but why?

THE HALLS OUTSIDE THE CAMPUS AUDITORIUM BUZZED WITH people who'd arrived for the ceremony. According to the program, the event should last about two hours and included a distribution of awards to instructors in five departments.

Layla happened to see Omar almost as soon as they arrived, which wasn't hard, considering his height and size. She waved to get his attention and rushed over.

"Hey, how're you doing?" She gave him a quick hug and an air kiss.

"Nervous, as if I'm the one getting the award," he replied with a hearty, deep-throated laugh.

"This should be nothing for you," she teased, alluding to his former career.

A former linebacker for the Atlanta Falcons, he had the meaty body to prove it. Since his days of playing professional football had been over for a while, he wasn't as big but maintained a similar physique and looked like he was about to pop out of the jacket that he wore over a white T-shirt.

"I'm nervous for Dana. She kept complaining that she hated having to wear heels and hoped she didn't trip when she walked across the stage."

"That's because you're looking out for our girl. You brought her here, right?"

"Yeah, and you know how she is. She hates the attention, but I told her she wasn't allowed to skip tonight."

"Good for you. Tamika and I told her the same thing. By the way, this is Rashad. I'm his better half."

"Damn," Rashad said, as Omar laughed.

Layla smiled sweetly and hugged Rashad's arm. "Rashad, this is Omar, a good friend of Dana's."

"I know who you are," Rashad said. "You used to play for the Falcons."

"Sure did. Feels like a lifetime ago."

"But it hasn't been that long. Nice to meet you, man."

"Good to meet you too."

They shook hands.

"I played football in high school. Running back," Rashad said, surprising Layla.

He'd never mentioned that before, and she tucked away that information about him. Rashad struck a pose, as if he had a football tucked under his arm. The three of them laughed.

Rashad appeared fine now, but on the ride over, the way he had released and gripped the steering wheel in quick succession revealed his tension.

"You ever go to the games here?" Omar asked.

"When I can."

"You gotta let me hook you up. Box seats."

"Oh damn, you're speaking my love language. I can't turn that down. I'm definitely interested," Rashad said.

"Cool." Omar turned to Layla. "Where's the little one?" he asked, referring to Tamika.

"I'm sure she'll be here soon. Oh, speak of the devil."

Tamika came sashaying toward them with her fiancé, Anton, beside her.

"Hey!" she said, with her usual bubbly personality, giving Omar a hug.

Tamika and Rashad greeted each other, and Anton and Rashad were introduce.

"Now that we're all here, and everyone knows everyone now, let's get inside before the ceremony starts," Layla said.

"After you," Omar said, extending a hand.

Tamika and Layla led the way into the auditorium, half filled with family, friends, and faculty and staff from the college. They found seats in the same aisle, and within a few minutes, the lights were turned down and the emcee approached the mic.

She greeted everyone with a welcoming smile and explained the purpose of the night was to honor the instructors from each department for their outstanding work and dedication. The president of the college came up and said a few words, and then the awards distribution commenced.

Before each teacher received their award, the emcee spoke briefly about their accomplishments and discussed how many years they had been working in their field. When it was Dana's turn, they talked about her work in the community, as well as the high praise she received from students and her fellow faculty members. The fact that she was one of the younger winners made her award that much sweeter. When they announced her name, Layla and the other four jumped to their feet, hollering and clapping.

"We're so proud of you!" Tamika yelled above the noise.

Omar put his fingers in his mouth and whistled. With her dreadlocks piled on her head, Dana remained calm, a serene smile on her face. She glanced in their direction and acknowledged them with a wider grin, before going back to her seat.

Right before the end of the ceremony, a special leadership award was announced. The winner of that award was unknown, and the president of the college returned to the stage to present it.

"The Michael Boldt Leadership Award goes to the faculty member who has most demonstrated exemplary leadership ability. This person is a great communicator and dependable collaborator among his or her peers. The award includes a $10,000 cash prize, additional teaching and research resources, as well as reimbursement for attending conferences and seminars for professional development. It's with great pleasure that I announce to you that tonight's winner of the Michael Boldt Leadership Award goes to English Instructor Dana Lindstrom."

Layla and Tamika gasped and jumped to their feet, clapping loudly for their friend. A shell-shocked Dana slowly returned to the stage as the president read a list of all the accomplishments that factored into her winning the award.

Layla didn't hear a word he said, too busy hugging Tamika and then clapping along with the rest of the audience. The night had turned out better than expected, and she was glad to be in attendance to support her friend.

After the ceremony, the crew of five surrounded Dana, giving her hugs and kisses and congratulations.

Omar lifted her from the ground in a bear hug and gave her a big smack on the cheek. "Proud of you, babe," he said in his deep voice.

"Thank you."

Amazingly, Dana blushed. She never blushed. Tamika and Layla glanced at each other, silently communicating that they'd tease her about her behavior later.

"I'm ready to get my drink on. Where are we going to celebrate?" Omar asked, rubbing his hands together.

"What's everybody in the mood for?" Anton asked. He stood behind Tamika with an arm looped around her neck, and she leaned back into him.

"I want a Long Island iced tea and some good music, that's it," Dana said, hugging her awards to her chest. The first was a framed certificate, and the leadership award was made of glass and shaped like a diamond, with her name etched in a gold plaque on the wooden base.

"How about Avery's Juke Joint?" Tamika suggested.

"I haven't been there in a long time. Is it still jumping?" Omar asked.

"Always. We might have to call ahead to get a table because it stays packed," Dana said.

"Let me handle that part." Omar pulled out his phone and walked away.

"It's nice to have a celebrity in our midst," Tamika said.

Rashad cleared his throat. "I hate to be a killjoy, but I'm not going to be able to join you at Avery's."

Layla stared at him. "Why not?"

Rashad's eyes shifted around the room before landing on Dana. "I have a lot of work to do at the office still. I wish I could hang."

"Oh no, that's too bad," Dana said.

"Yeah, I'm really sorry about this."

He sounded sincere, but Layla couldn't help but wonder what work he'd left unfinished at the office that required him to bail on the evening he'd assured her he had time for.

"Nice to meet you," Anton said, and they gave each other some dap.

"Likewise."

"Thanks for coming tonight. I really appreciate it," Dana said.

"I wanted to be supportive. Congratulations again. I'll see you later." He kissed Layla's temple.

She swallowed her disappointment, wanting to pull him aside and question him but thought better of it. Faking happiness, she overlaid her concerned, frowning face with a happy one and said, "See you later."

Rashad's troubled gaze met hers for a moment, and he seemed about to say something, but then he grinned, giving her one of his typical Rashad expressions. The outgoing, devil-may-care look where he flashed his pearly whites, as brilliant as the diamonds that sparkled in his ears. Then he was gone, winding his way out of the auditorium between the disappearing crowd.

Her girlfriends came to stand on either side of her.

"Is everything okay?" Dana asked quietly.

"I hope so," Layla replied.

❧ 19 ☙

Rashad knocked twice and then barged into Alex's office without waiting for an answer. His friend looked up from the computer with a surprised expression.

"You have a minute?" Rashad asked.

"Sure."

Rashad shut the door. "He's started again." He tossed the opened envelope on the desk.

Alex read the front and then leaned back in his chair. "He used your old name."

"Yeah. Asshole."

"What does he want?"

"To make my life hell, what else? I should have never reached out to him." He rubbed the back of his neck, aching from the amount of tension he'd been carrying with no relief since last night.

After Heather's death, he reached out to his father at the George Beto Unit, a men's maximum-security prison in Texas. At first he thought his father might have changed, but within months he freed Rashad of the notion that he had been rehabilitated. Rashad cut off all contact, and the envelope yesterday was the first time he'd heard from him since then.

"He's your father. It's not surprising that at some point you would reach out to him. Why did he contact you again?"

"He sent me what I asked for. Pictures of my mother. Pictures of me from when I was a kid. Remember how he refused to give them to me? I started to doubt he even had them, but he had them all along, son of a bitch." Bitter anger consumed him and spilled over into his voice. He hadn't felt this way in a long time and hated that the old feelings had re-emerged.

Alex opened the envelope and removed some of the photos and flipped through them. As Rashad watched, his stomach tightened with tension and nausea roiled in his stomach. He wished he didn't have any connection to Chester Reddick.

Last night when he left Layla and her friends, he'd gone back to the condo, opened the package and flipped through the photos. All sorts of emotions—anger, nostalgia, sadness—overwhelmed him, and more than anything he'd wanted to spill his guts to Layla. How many times had he told himself that he wouldn't, couldn't allow himself to need anyone? Not even Layla. He'd needed her last night—needed to tell her how much he was hurting and tell her the truth about his father so she could help him carry this burden he didn't want to bear, but he couldn't—because he'd lied to her. He had told her his parents were dead, but they weren't.

When she came home, he'd pretended to be asleep, and this morning he left early before she woke up.

"In the letter he said I didn't deserve them since I was the reason he was in prison in the first place, but he sent them anyway to prove that he wasn't the bad person I thought he was. A good will gesture. Then he asked for money again."

"*Dios*, I'm sorry, Rashad." Alex's hazel eyes filled with sympathy. He knew all about Chester Reddick and the pain he'd caused not only to Rashad, but to a large number of women.

"At least I have the pictures I wanted." That was the silver lining.

Thirteen-year-old Rashad had been the one to find the bloodied clothes tucked away in the garage, as well as a pair of earrings that matched the description of a woman he'd seen missing on the news. He'd already suspected that his father was up to no good on the nights he left him home alone, and seeing those items convinced him to call the police.

When his father had been arrested, Rashad had been removed from the home, and the entire house was off limits because it was considered a crime scene. Years later, Rashad realized he had no photos of himself as a kid, and that need to connect to the past niggled at the back of his mind for a long time. When he contacted his father in prison, he'd asked about any photos he still had, and he'd tagged on a request about his mother—Ernestine Reddick.

"Layla saw the package and asked me about the name on the envelope. I think I put her off, but I'm not sure." Rashad paced the floor, rubbing a hand across the back of his neck, annoyed by the constant tension there.

"Why didn't you tell her the truth?"

"The truth? That my father was a serial rapist who killed his last victim, and the only reason I'm here is because he raped my mother? That the name Rashad Greene is one I cobbled together after I turned eighteen so I wouldn't have any connection to a monster? I'm sure she would have taken that very well."

Alex sighed and stuffed the pictures back in the envelope. "You told me you're in love with her, and she's practically living at your condo these days. Don't you think it's time you tell her everything?"

Rashad rested his butt against the credenza and laughed. "Yeah, that's so easy to do."

Alex stood. "Aren't you the one who told me I should tell Sherry the truth about me and Heather? Now is the time to take your own advice."

"Your situation was different, Alex. Sherry had to get used to the idea of you and Heather, but there's no way Layla is going to be okay with this. I told her my parents were dead, meanwhile my mother is alive and well in Huntsville, Alabama and probably doesn't want to have anything to do with me, and my father is in a maximum-security prison for brutalizing more than twenty women over the span of a decade. How do you think she's going to look at me, when she comes from a pristine family of lawyers and politicians? You think she'll jump at the chance to be with a man whose background is so dirty? She won't want the stink on her." His jaw and throat tightened at the thought of Layla's scorn. There were so many other men out there without his baggage that he couldn't fathom her wanting to remain in his life and plan a future with him when she learned the truth.

"You know her better than I do, but I've never seen you behave this way about anyone else. You used to laugh at the idea of The One, and I think Layla is your One. You need to secure this relationship before she finds out you lied and everything blows up in your face."

"I need more time."

"For what? To come up with more lies? Whether you tell her now or tell her later, the result will be the same. You're putting off the inevitable."

"Then so be it, but I don't think I can manage anything else right now." Rashad pushed away from the credenza and picked up the envelope.

"I hope you know what you're doing."

"I don't, but I can't risk losing her again." Losing Layla would be a nightmare come true.

Rashad exited the office.

"Layla!"

Hearing her name yelled, Layla almost jumped out of the seat in front of Ethan's desk. "I'm sorry, what did you say?"

She didn't have much of an attention span and unfortunately

had been drifting off during their conversation. A huge no-no for someone like Ethan, who paid a premium for her time and attention.

He pinched the bridge of his nose. "Is there something else you'd rather be doing?" he asked.

"No, I'm sorry. I have a lot on my mind." Of course, that was no excuse.

"Do you think you could set it aside for the next few minutes while we're talking? After we're done, you're welcome to go back to whatever daydreams you're having."

The biting comment made heat rise in her cheeks.

"No problem," Layla muttered. She couldn't even be mad at him because she was screwing up. She straightened in the chair and poised her stylus pen above the blank page on her iPad.

Ethan continued. "I need you to travel to Miami with me this weekend. You'll only have to stay Saturday night. Can you make it?"

"Yes, that's no problem."

"Good. Coordinate transportation and flights with Daria," he said.

"Okay. No problem." She wrote herself a note.

Ethan studied her for a beat. "What's going on with you?"

Layla pasted a bright smile on her face. "Nothing. Everything is fine."

"Everything is not fine, but I certainly hope it will be. I need you at 100 percent, Layla. Whatever you're going through, please fix it before you come to Miami. You know how much I depend on you."

"I do. Not to worry."

"Good. That's all I have. You can leave. I have a dinner meeting, so I'll leave now too." He glanced at his watch and stood. "I'll see you tomorrow on the plane."

He grabbed his briefcase and exited the office, but Layla remained seated. She had to get her act together. She didn't think Ethan would fire her, but he had a low tolerance for incompetence. It's just that she couldn't think right now. All her brain cells were preoccupied with thoughts of Rashad and that package she picked up yesterday. Then of course, there was his unexpected departure from Dana's award ceremony and his early morning departure—before she even woke up. He must have left at the crack of dawn.

Something was wrong, and in usual Rashad fashion, he wouldn't share that with her. Well, if he was going to keep information from her, as well as obviously lie, she had no choice but to do her own investigation. She'd put that off so far because a sixth sense warned if she went poking around in his affairs, she would find something she didn't want to find. She had no choice, however, because curiosity gnawed at her constantly, and Rashad was not forthcoming with information.

To begin her search, she typed "Deshawn Reddick" into the search field on the Internet. The name was unusual enough that only a single page of results popped up. She scanned the images and halted when she came to one of a dark-skinned young man wearing a football uniform in an old photo.

She froze. She didn't want to continue because her suspicions were about to be confirmed. Closing her eyes, she took a deep breath before clicking on the link below the photo and was taken to an article from a small paper in Texas. She skimmed the piece, which praised the athleticism of the young running back who'd scored the winning touchdown that won Lee High School the state championship.

The young man smiled happily into the camera, though she detected sadness in his eyes. Her gaze remained glued to the photo. Deshawn Reddick looked exactly like Rashad. In fact, there was no doubt in her mind that he was a younger Rashad. Which meant...

Layla yanked air into her lungs with a deep inhale.

Deshawn Reddick was Rashad Greene. Rashad Greene was Deshawn Reddick.

If all of that was true, why had he never mentioned it? Why had he pretended he didn't know the name Deshawn Reddick?

Layla's hand lifted to her mouth in shock.

Who the hell was she sleeping with?

🎕 20 🎕

When Rashad entered his condo, soft music was playing, and the lights were dimmed. Layla sat on the sofa with her legs curled under her, reading a book.

"Hey," he said by way of greeting.

She closed the book and set it on the table beside the sofa. "Hey. Have you eaten? I picked up a lasagna from La Tavola Italiano, in case you were hungry. It's in the refrigerator."

She was always thinking about him, making sure that he was taken care of.

"I ate at the office," Rashad replied.

He bent to greet her with a kiss, but she turned away and stood.

"Something wrong?"

"No, I'm tired, that's all. Tomorrow I'm flying to Miami with Ethan, and I'll be spending the night there and coming back on Sunday." She wouldn't look at him, and her voice sounded stiff.

"Okay."

He'd come a long way since their first relationship, when he didn't trust Ethan at all. He'd finally accepted the man was her boss, nothing more. The bigger concern was Layla's mood. He didn't know how to tell Layla about his past and admit to the lies he'd told. He needed time to think, plan, strategize. Blurt out everything or ease her into it? He wasn't sure.

"I'm going to take a shower and then go to bed. I'm tired," he said.

"You left early this morning," Layla remarked.

"I had to handle some things at work." Rashad went into the bedroom, avoiding eye contact so he wouldn't have to look at her when he lied again.

He removed his jacket and tossed it on the chair in front of the bed.

"The winery again?"

He turned to face Layla. He hadn't been aware that she had followed him into the bedroom.

"Yes, minor details that need to be ironed out. Nothing too serious," he replied.

"So it's basically a done deal then?"

"Pretty much."

He turned his back to her as he unbuttoned his shirt. He tossed that on the chair, as well, standing in his undershirt and slacks as he removed his shoes.

"I lied," Layla said.

He swung to face her. "About what?"

"When you asked if something was wrong, I lied when I said there was nothing wrong, and that I was just tired."

"Look, if you're upset about my leaving you and your friends last night, I'll make it up to you. I had a lot to take care of at the office, and—"

"Now *you're* lying." She spoke in a matter-of-fact voice, quiet, simply looking at him.

He wasn't sure how to take her mood. "What do you mean?"

"While I was at Avery's, I called here and spoke to Liam. He told me that you had returned to the building and were upstairs. So then, the only question I have is, why lie? Why pretend that you went back to work? Did you not want to hang out with me and my friends?"

"No, that's not why." He started walking toward her.

"I know that's not why. I also know that the reason you came back was because you wanted to look at the contents of that envelope." She spoke in matter-of-fact tones, not raising her voice, but he sensed the heightened emotions behind the words.

"I don't know what you're talking about."

"Stop it. Stop lying to me right now! Stop treating me like I'm stupid."

"I'm not treating you like you're stupid. I had to stop by to pick up some things before I went into the office. That doesn't mean I lied to you."

Clutching her head in exasperation, Layla said, "I can't believe you're doing this again. I can't believe you're really going to stand there and lie to me, when you know good and well you didn't leave this condo after you came up. Do I need to ask the manager for the security tape? If I do, will you just come up with another lie? Another excuse?"

"I'm done talking to you because you're acting hysterical." Rashad set off for the bathroom.

"I know who Deshawn Reddick is," she called out.

Goose bumps popped out on Rashad's skin, and he stopped moving. Tension pounded his neck and shoulders. Slowly, he faced Layla, his heart tripling the rate of its normal beating.

Tears shimmered in her eyes. "You."

He didn't say a word, waiting to see how much she knew.

"Nothing to say?" she asked.

"I don't know what you want me to say," he replied in a low voice.

She laughed, a bitter, caustic sound that conveyed her exasperation and fatigue. "At least you didn't deny it. Why didn't you tell me?"

"You don't have to know everything about me, Layla."

She laughed again. "Thank you for that, because I was this close to falling for your bullshit again. I can't do this anymore."

Fear raged in his heart. "Do what? Of course you have every right—"

"No, you meant what you said, and once again your honesty has opened my eyes and made me realize where I stand with you, which is nowhere."

"Don't say that."

"Why not? It's true."

"I love you!"

Her eyebrows flew higher, and she bit her lip as she struggled to keep from crying. "I'm not falling for that."

She went into the closet, and he watched in horror as she pulled out her suitcase and the bags filled with clothes and shoes she'd purchased the day before.

"What are you doing?"

"I told you, I'm done."

"You act like I'm so closed off, when I'm not. I've shared plenty with you this time around. You know Alex and know about Heather. I told you about my foster parents and my life on my own. What more do you want?"

"I want all of you," Layla said.

"This is all I can give you right now."

"Well that's not enough," she snapped.

"So you're just gonna leave me?"

"What else is there to do, Rashad?" she screamed, eyes wild with anger. "You don't listen. You don't care."

"That's not true!"

"You keep me close when it suits you and push me away when it doesn't. I feel like I'm a yo-yo with you. Up and down, up and down, over and over again. I'm going crazy and I can't take it anymore. I can't take *this* anymore. *I don't know who you are!*" She took a tremulous breath and blinked rapidly. "It's over. For good this time. I can't... I can't be with you."

"And I can't be without you," he bit out. Those words cost

him dearly. He struggled under their weight. "It's not easy for me to open up myself. I could be mocked or ridiculed or rejected. It's not easy."

"Why would I do that to you?"

"I don't know. I..." His throat closed, and his voice shut off.

"You and your trust issues." She pointed a white-tipped fingernail at him. "Tell you what, when you figure out what you really want, then go get her. Stop playing these stupid games and giving stupid excuses."

She dialed a number on her phone, and when the person on the other end picked up, she said, "I'm ready. I'm leaving." Then she hung up.

"Who the hell was that?" Rashad demanded.

"Tamika and Dana were waiting in the parking lot. Depending on how this conversation went, I told them I would be leaving, and since it went exactly as I expected, they're coming to help me."

She rushed around, grabbing clothes and stuffing them into the suitcase. He watched with a mixture of despair and detachment. She was going to leave him. He should do something to stop her, yet he felt incapable of moving or putting forth the simplest effort.

"I have a lot of baggage," he said by way of explanation. That's all he could muster. Only his mouth could move.

"Everybody does." She slammed the suitcase shut and struggled to close it because all her garments had been stuffed in without any respect to order or neatness.

Rashad didn't help her. He wanted her to fail. The longer she struggled, the longer she stayed in the condo with him.

That moment didn't last. She eventually sat on the suitcase and snapped the locks closed. Then she hauled it off the bed and dragged it by the wheels into the living room. Rashad followed more slowly and watched her take her other bags out there, too, but he refused to help her.

The doorbell rang, and she rushed to open it. Layla snatched open the door, and her two girlfriends were standing there. Tamika pulled her close, enveloping her in a protective embrace while glaring at Rashad over her friend's shoulder.

Dana wouldn't look at him. She went around the other two and picked up one of the bags and grasped the handle of the suitcase. "All of these?" she asked.

Layla brushed tears from her eyes and nodded. Her watery eyes stared at him as she swiped under her nose.

"Layla." Rashad took a few tentative steps forward.

Tamika grabbed the other two bags in one hand and touched Layla's shoulder. "Let's get out of here."

He read hesitation in Layla's face. Yes, she was angry. Hurt. But she didn't want to leave. This was his chance to change her mind, but he didn't say a word. All he had to do was tell her why he'd changed his name. She was waiting for him to say something —anything—that would make her change her mind. Yet he held his mouth closed. She picked up her Chanel purse from the coffee table, and he watched as she walked out with her friends and shut the door.

Rashad put a hand to his pounding head. She was gone.

He marched over to the door and hit it. Over and over he slammed the heel of both hands against the sturdy oak, sending pain like lightning bolts zigzagging up his arms. When the pain became too much, he stopped and rested his forehead against the door.

"Layla," he whispered. "Fuck."

He'd wanted to stop her but couldn't.

Because she deserved better.

Tapping his finger on the table, Rashad sat by the window watching, waiting. Layla had gone into the Coffee Cup earlier, and soon she'd be coming out. Lucky for him, her routine hadn't changed. She still went there for breakfast on Saturday mornings. He'd parked far away so she wouldn't see his yellow Porsche and had already paid for his coffee so he could leave and catch her as she returned home.

He'd had a lot of time to think, and he'd panicked at the thought of losing Layla again, which had caused him to make poor decisions. Lying and hiding his past from her had been the wrong moves. Since she left him two weeks ago, he walked around with a permanent headache. Every now and again the pain went away, but it always came back, like someone suffering from withdrawal. That's exactly what being without her felt like —withdrawal.

He only slept a few hours each night, if at all. Often, he lay in bed wide awake, and to keep from going crazy, he'd get his tablet and watch a movie or sit in the living room and watch TV. He was restless and irritable, and baking—his usual go-to activity to bring him peace—didn't provide much relief. At least the office staff benefited from the sweets he made.

He had sent a letter to his father, thanking him for the photos but reminding him he had no intention of sending him more money or keeping in touch. He hadn't received a reply and didn't know if he would, but he'd already instructed Liam that he should refuse any more packages that came for Deshawn Reddick, and he instructed the mail carrier not to place letters addressed to Deshawn in his box. Deshawn Reddick no longer existed. Rashad Greene had replaced him almost fifteen years ago.

His gaze snapped to a flash of pink, and he saw Layla walk down the sidewalk. He held his breath. The shock of seeing her kept him immobile for several seconds before he regained the wherewithal to act. Exiting the donut shop, he looked both ways before jogging across the street and walking up beside her.

"Hi, Layla."

She caught her breath and stared at him in shock.

They hadn't seen each other in two weeks, and he hated to acknowledge she looked great. Fantastic, even. Fresh-faced in gold-frame glasses and an up do with no makeup on. The pink joggers and pink T-shirt molded to her curves. She looked cute and sexy as hell, as if nothing was amiss on this fine spring morning. Meanwhile his life was like a city that had been repeatedly bombed, with nothing left behind but empty wasteland.

"I don't want to talk to you, Rashad."

"I know." He stuffed his hands in the pockets of his chinos. "But I'm hoping to change your mind."

"You can't."

She picked up the pace and averted her eyes from him. Her cheeks flushed crimson in agitation, but he couldn't simply walk away. He'd come here with the express purpose of baring his soul.

"Would you hear me out?"

She swung to face him, lips pressed together in anger. "Why? So you can lie to me or pretend that you've changed yet again? Or from the look on your face, maybe this time you have a sob story that'll make me feel sorry for you. No, I'm not doing this with you now or later. You had your chance to prove to me that you've changed. I was satisfied with us having sex occasionally, but *you* changed the dynamics of our relationship. *You* demanded more while holding back. I don't have to listen to you. I said everything I needed to say when I left your condo two weeks ago."

"I know I fucked up."

"Yes, you did. Again."

"Yes, again, but I have a good explanation. I need to tell you everything. It's eating me up that you think the reason we didn't work out is because of something you did."

She laughed shrilly, as if he'd made the funniest joke in the world. "Oh no, is that what you think? Please, rest easy that I'm confident the reason we're not together has nothing to do with my actions. That's all on you. I wanted you to let me in, but guess what? I no longer care. You can go along with a clear conscience to the next woman. Maybe you'll learn from all of this and understand you can't keep hiding who you are. For all I know, you might be a rapist and that's why you changed your name and won't share your past with me."

Rashad winced. She was much closer to the truth than she realized, and a sinking sensation swarmed behind his abs. Maybe this was a mistake. He wanted to turn and flee, but how could he, when his future was standing directly in front of him?

She might say she didn't care, but he saw the hurt in her eyes and heard the pain in her voice. No matter how perfectly put together the package, Layla was no freer of her feelings for him than he was of his feelings for her. They were still bound together, and she loved him, or at least cared about him. That much he knew without a doubt. He could build on that.

"I only need five minutes of your time, and then I'll leave."

Layla vigorously shook her head. "You're not listening, and I don't know how else to tell you. I'm done, Rashad. Fed up. When a woman's fed up, there's nothing you can say or do to change her mind. I'm moving on with my life, and you should do the same."

She moved quickly away from him and into the building, and Rashad didn't follow. He stood on the empty sidewalk, arms hanging loosely at his sides in a sort of surrender.

He couldn't reach her. The look in her eyes and the despondent tone all pointed to not only a lack of interest, she simply didn't care, like she said. She might love him, but she no longer liked him. She no longer wanted him in her life, and the brutality of that rejection was worse than anything he could have ever imagined.

Layla was his life. His everything. And this time, he'd lost her for good.

HUGGING HERSELF, LAYLA SAT ON THE WINDOWSILL OF HER loft. Tamika and Dana were there, too, seated on the comfy sofa in front of the coffee table with vegan food—something new they were trying—spread out on the table before them. She didn't have much of an appetite because she couldn't stop thinking about her conversation with Rashad earlier.

"He didn't look like himself," she said to her friends.

"What do you mean?" Tamika asked, spooning vegetarian curry over the rice on her plate.

"He looked sad. I've never seen him like that before. I've seen Rashad upset, cocky, amused... Everything you can imagine. I've never ever seen him sad." She didn't want to care, but his appearance pulled at her heartstrings. She still loved him and couldn't simply turn off her feelings like switching off a faucet.

She and her friends remained quiet for a while, and then Dana broke the silence.

"What do you want to do?"

Layla buried her face in her hands and let out a little scream. "I don't know! I know that I don't want to get back together with him, but I'm a little concerned about his appearance. He didn't look well. He didn't look like the Rashad I know."

"Sounds like he might be going through a tough spell, possibly because he misses you...?" Dana suggested.

"And if he does? That's not my fault. I've suffered, too, and I'm tired. I'm tired of being treated as if I'm not important, when he's everything to me." Her voice cracked, because simply talking about Rashad heightened her emotions. "Sometimes I feel like I'll never get over him," she said quietly.

Dana went over to the window sill and sat beside Layla. She put an arm across her shoulders. "You will. It takes time, that's all."

She nodded. Then she looked at Tamika. "You're awfully quiet."

"Because neither of you are going to like what I have to say."

"Say what you're thinking," Layla said.

Tamika pursed her lips. "I think you should hear him out."

Dana sighed dramatically.

Tamika set down her plate. "Look, I'll be the first to admit that I never cared for Rashad when you got involved with him the first time. I thought he was too slick, too suave, and when you started dating Elijah, I considered him Rashad number two, which made me uneasy. With Rashad back in your life, and based on what you said a second ago, I think you should give him another chance. Maybe not for a relationship, but at least hear his explanation. You'll never forgive yourself if you don't."

"I don't know him, Tamika. His name's not Rashad. What else is he hiding, and do I want to know?"

"Maybe, maybe not. He came here to tell you something, and it sounds like it's the explanation you've been waiting for. Aren't you at least curious to know what he has to say?"

"I don't like this," Dana muttered.

"Dana, I'm not suggesting she start screwing him again, but she should find out his reason for lying. If nothing else, for closure."

Dana shook her head. "You guys know my policy. When I'm done with a man, I'm done. Closure is tricky. Closure will have you in his bed, on your back, with your legs wide open in the air, wondering how you got there."

Tamika snorted, and Layla laughed at Dana's pessimistic but vivid imagination.

"You laugh, but I'm serious. Forget closure and preserve your sanity. Rashad has shown you he hasn't changed in all this time. *Three years.* What could he possibly say that would make a difference?"

"The fact that he's different," Tamika said. "Layla said so herself, that he opened up more and no longer wanted a casual relationship. Look, you can do whatever you want to do. We're giving you conflicting advice, and you'll have to make the final decision yourself. What would put your mind at ease? Forget closure. Call it whatever you want, but I don't think you'll be satisfied with simply cutting him off this time. Not now that you know he's definitely keeping secrets, but is willing to open up and share what he didn't before."

Dana shrugged. "She's right. Ultimately, the decision is yours. You know what I think, but whatever you decide, we'll have your back."

"Thanks," Layla said gratefully. "I'll think about it, but honestly, I'm leaning toward ignoring Rashad—or whatever his name is—and simply leaving things the way they are. As far as I'm concerned, nothing he could say would change my mind at this point. He's had two chances and failed both times. It's too late."

Layla went over to the table and started making herself a plate.

She sincerely hoped she wasn't lying to her friends... and to herself.

❧ 22 ❧

Layla had lied to herself. Big surprise. That's why she was standing outside Rashad's door a little more than twenty-four hours after she'd seen him.

Last night, she barely slept and stared up at the ceiling, thoughts constantly on Rashad and what he was doing. *How* he was doing. She came over unannounced with the intention of taking him by surprise but now didn't think that tactic was a good idea.

"I should have called first," she muttered, turning away.

The door swung open, and she froze like a deer in headlights. Rashad looked dressed to go out in basketball shorts and an aquamarine men's running tank. The sleeveless shirt showed off his muscular biceps, wiry forearms, and he smelled good, too, as if he'd recently showered. She bit back a moan of feminine appreciation.

"Hi."

He stared at her as if she were an alien being. "What are you doing here?"

"I don't know," she replied with a nervous laugh, tucking her hair behind her left ear. "I know better, and... no, that's a lie. I do know why I'm here. I came to hear your explanation."

"Oh." He blinked, as if snapping out of a trance. "Er... come in." He stepped back, continuing to stare, stunned by her appearance.

She walked into the familiar space that after two short weeks and their emotion-charged parting didn't feel familiar anymore. "If you're going out, I could come back."

"No, I was going to meet Alex and Sherry at the park, but I'll let them know I can't come. Have a seat and give me a sec."

She sat on the edge of the sofa while he sent a text. Afterward, he took a seat in the armchair, rested his elbows on his knees, and simply looked at her. "It's good to see you, sweetness."

Her chest hurt with nostalgia to hear him call her by the familiar endearment, but she pushed aside her feelings. "I want the truth, Rashad."

"I'll give you the truth."

Layla rubbed her hands up and down her thighs. "I don't want you to get the wrong idea. This isn't us getting back together. I came here to understand why you lied to me, and why you changed your name to Rashad."

"Okay," he said, nodding. He took a deep breath and released it. "Well, you know my real name is not Rashad Greene. It is now, legally, but when I was born, my name was Deshawn Reddick. To explain how I got to this point, I need to start from the beginning, way back, to when my parents met." He took another deep breath and let it out slowly. "My father, Chester Reddick, was a quiet man, kept mostly to himself but had a good-paying job. He met my mother at the local YMCA. She worked there, and he had a membership and used the gym. They started dating and eventually got married, but their relationship was rocky, and my mother decided she was going to leave him. My dad wasn't having that. They fought constantly, and one night... he raped her."

Layla gasped.

Rashad rubbed his hands together, staring at the carpet. "She had me, but um... she didn't stay. She left me with my father and moved from Texas to Alabama where she had family."

Rashad continued with the story, telling her that while his father wasn't cruel, he wasn't affectionate, and Rashad longed to gain his approval. He excelled in football, thinking that would make his father show interest in him, but he didn't. Around the time he was twelve years old, reports of a serial rapist had the city on edge. His M.O. indicated he was targeting prostitutes and women considered loners, without family or close ties. A Black male was the only solid description they had.

Rashad became preoccupied with this criminal and, through his own research, noticed that on all the nights the attacks occurred, his father had left him home alone. Pure speculation, but he became suspicious of his father, and when he found Chester's blood-stained clothes in the garage, he called the police.

"Oh my god." Layla's brow wrinkled, and she covered her mouth with both hands. "That must have been very difficult to do."

"It was. I didn't know if I was doing the right thing, and if I was wrong, my relationship with my father would be irretrievably broken, but I wasn't wrong. They eventually found the body of that last woman, and DNA connected him to the rapes of the others. Twenty-two women over the course of ten years.

"After Heather passed, I thought about him a lot and reached out to him. I don't know what possessed me to do that. We hadn't communicated in almost 20 years, ever since he went to prison. Maybe I wanted family and needed to know how he was doing. Maybe it was unresolved guilt for calling the police all those years ago. Whatever the reason, it was a mistake."

"Why?" Layla asked softly.

"He didn't care about me," he said simply. "We exchanged letters and talked. At first he referred to me as Deshawn—on the phone, in correspondence—but I kept reminding him that I was Rashad now. Then he started asking me for money. Initially I didn't care and didn't mind because I thought we were developing a relationship. I'd finally gotten his attention and, I thought, his love. Warped, I know.

"He began asking for more money and more frequently. I figured out pretty quickly that my need to connect with him wasn't reciprocated when I asked him about any photos he had of me and my mother, and he said he'd give them to me for a price. That's when I really knew he didn't give a damn about me."

"Oh no," Layla whispered.

"That's what was in the envelope the other day—the photos that I asked for. For whatever reason, he changed his mind. But I knew last year that he was using me and playing with my emotions because I missed having a father figure in my life and longed for that type of normal relationship. Once I realized what he was doing, I told him I was done. Then I cut him off."

"How did he take that?"

He smiled wryly. "Not well. He sent a pretty nasty letter, accused me of thinking that I was better than him, and more or less cursed me out. Even reminded me that I was the reason he was in prison. I thought that was the end of hearing from him until you picked up the package from Liam."

"He was back to calling you Deshawn again."

"That was a dig at me. When I turned eighteen, I changed my name to Rashad. A fresh start, and... I didn't want any connection to my father. Rashad was the name of my football coach in high school. Greene was the last name of my foster parents—Joe and Suzanne, who moved to California. My father never liked that I'd changed my name, and by addressing the letter to Deshawn, he was reminding me of who I was, forcing me to face the fact that he was my father. He didn't want me to forget."

Rashad stood restlessly, rubbing a hand across the back of his

neck. "Personality-wise, we're nothing alike, by design. I became
the anti-Chester, made sure I was the opposite of him—a serious, uptight loner. He hated women, I loved them. He flew
under the radar and didn't bring attention to himself. I wanted
attention, was outgoing, and had lots of friends. I wanted to
stand out."

"Is your mother still alive?"

Rashad nodded. "I went through a period of being bitter and
angry that she left me with him, but over time, it no longer
mattered. Five years ago I found her in Alabama. I have a
younger sister from her second marriage that ended in divorce."

"What did she say?"

He shook his head, pursing his lips. "I never talked to her.
Didn't have the guts."

Her heart broke. "You thought she would reject you."

"Yeah," he said quietly.

Layla studied her nails before asking, "Why didn't you tell me
all this before?"

Rashad shrugged carelessly. "You come from a good,
upstanding family. Your parents are well-known attorneys. Your
siblings all hold jobs in important professions—attorney, judge,
politician. When people learn about my background, that will
reflect negatively on you and could affect your family's
reputation."

Layla stood up. "I disagree. If there is one thing people love,
it's the story of the underdog and how he overcame. You overcame a tough upbringing. You were on your own at sixteen, you
put yourself through college, you have your own business, and
you're about to embark on another one. That's what I would call
a success. You're a success story, Rashad. You turned out okay.
Better than okay."

He looked at her with stark confusion in his face. "I didn't
run around telling everybody my story, but I told Alex and
Heather because I needed to tell someone. I needed to share the
burden that I had been carrying by myself. They didn't judge me,

and we stayed friends. The three of us knew everything about each other because we didn't have anyone else. Their understanding gave me a false sense of comfort. I believed that other people would be as understanding, and I shared my story with a woman I was involved with.

"I'll never forget the look on her face. She didn't express disgust or leave right away, but she definitely changed. I saw it in her eyes and the way she looked at me for the rest of the night. One of those emotions was fear, Layla. She became afraid of me, and that... that might have hurt more than anything else. Because that was my biggest fear, that when people saw me, they would see Chester Reddick too. She left early that night, and I never saw her again."

"I'm sorry you went through that, but you're not your father, and you shouldn't have to pay for his crimes," Layla said fiercely.

Brow furrowed, Rashad's jaw tightened. "I don't see the same emotions on your face. You're still here."

Layla moved closer but stopped when she noticed the tension in his body. "Why would I leave?"

"Aren't you worried? You know the truth now. You're not afraid of me? You're not afraid of tarnishing your family's name?"

She shrugged. "Nothing I know now changes my opinion of you. I love you, Rashad, and... I guess I'm not going anywhere. Everything I want is here. I'm all in..." Her voice trembled. "If you'll have me."

"If I'll have you?" Rashad closed the gap between them and gently took her head between his hands. "I've always wanted you, but I've been so damn scared. That's hard for me to admit. More than once Alex has called me out, and I've denied being afraid." He finally smiled, a genuine one that didn't necessarily filter into his eyes, but demonstrated that he was coming around. "When you asked about the name on the package, I panicked. Lying about my past had become a reflex, for self-preservation. Your question was the perfect opportunity to tell you everything, and I blew it. I'm sorry, sweetness. I just love you so damn much, I couldn't risk losing you again. I'm not complete without you. So yes, I'll have you. For as long as you'll have me."

She gave him a watery smile, stroking his jaw with her thumb. "Then you're stuck with me indefinitely, Mr. Greene, because I'm not going anywhere."

She raised up onto her toes and gently kissed his lips.

❧ 23 ❧

Layla had missed the comfort of lying in Rashad's arms during the weeks they were apart, so she took great pleasure in snuggling up to him in bed, head on his shoulder, one bare leg thrown across his thighs.

Earlier, after he'd bared his soul, they went out to eat and talked some more about his past. Free of the burden of shame, he opened up to her, and she devoured every morsel of information he willingly shared. Back at the condo, he showed her the photos his father sent, and for the first time she saw pictures of him as a child. One of him playing in the bathtub and another where he showed off his missing front teeth were among her favorites.

Coming here had been the right decision. Not only had they made up, but having him share all of himself deepened the intimacy between them.

Layla lifted onto one elbow. "Have you ever reconsidered contacting your mother?"

"A million times at least, and every time I stop myself because my reason for reaching out would be selfish. It's all about me and my needs, but I don't want to remind her of what happened. I can't do that to her."

Caressing his chest, Layla said, "It's been thirty-three years since she left, and she might have healed by now."

"If she has, I don't want to be the reason she relapses or starts having nightmares. My father raped her, and I look just like him, Layla. It would be cruel to do that to her."

"I'm not going to push you, but consider this a gentle prodding. You don't have to show up at her house unannounced. You could start by sending her a letter, introducing yourself, and seeing if she responds."

"If she doesn't, though…"

The unfinished sentence carried the heft of pain. Like so many abandoned children, Rashad worried that his mother didn't want to be found. Layla wasn't in his shoes and couldn't fathom his fears. She had a big, loving family, and they all got along well.

She didn't want to cause Rashad or his mother anymore pain. She rested her head on his shoulder. "I'm on your side, whatever you decide," she said quietly.

☙❧

"I CAN'T EAT ANOTHER BITE, I'M DONE," ALEX SAID, PATTING his belly. He was an attractive man, with wavy black hair, hazel eyes, and a light Colombian accent.

His wife, Sherry, sat next to him, visibly pregnant with her light brown skin glowing. During dinner Layla learned they were having a boy. Layla and Rashad sat across from them in the almost empty restaurant.

Coming here to celebrate the closing of the Lion Mountain Vineyards deal had been Alex's idea, and during the meal she clearly saw why he and Rashad were so close. They were very in sync business wise, but business wasn't the only topic of conversation during the night, and their love and affection for each other was obvious as they ribbed each other and shared inside jokes.

Sometimes Sherry joined in, but it was obvious the true bond was between the two men sitting across from each other, proving that family didn't necessarily mean blood relatives. Family was what you made it, with people who loved you and who you could depend on.

"Same. I can't eat another bite," Rashad said, letting his fork clatter onto the ceramic plate.

"Lightweights," Sherry said, slicing into her chocolate cake.

Alex slipped an arm behind her. "Sweetheart, you might be taking this eating for two thing too far."

Layla and Rashad groaned loudly to let Alex know he'd screwed up.

Sherry shot him a dirty look. "Excuse me?"

"Uh-oh. You better turn on that Colombian charm because you're in trouble now," Rashad said.

Layla rested a hand on his thigh, giggling as she sipped her wine.

"*Mi amor*, you know I'm only kidding," Alex said.

"You better be."

Alex cupped his wife's face and continuously pecked her lips until she started giggling and begged him to stop.

The waiter came by. "Can I get you anything else?" he asked.

"The check, please," Alex replied.

The waiter placed the black check folder on the table and walked away. Rashad snatched it up before Alex could.

"What are you doing?" Alex asked.

"Dinner's on me tonight."

"You don't have to do that," Alex said.

"Sure I do. Besides, if all goes well, I'll be making a lot of money with a vineyard I bought an hour from here." He flashed a grin and then lifted the bottle of wine from the table. "One more toast, before the night ends."

Rashad topped off all the glasses except Sherry's. They held their wine aloft, while she held up a glass of water.

"What are we toasting to?" Sherry asked.

"To success," Alex answered.

"To the support of family and friends," Rashad added.

"To love and new beginnings," Layla chimed in. Her gaze connected with Rashad's, and he took her hand under the table.

"Here, here," he said enthusiastically.

"Here, here!" Sherry and Alex added.

They all four clinked their glasses together.

❦ 24 ❦

Rashad had never been so nervous in his entire life.

Today was the day that he would meet his mother for the first time since he was a baby. The first time since she left him with his father thirty-three years ago. For the first time in all that time, they would lay eyes on each other, in person.

He and Layla sat in a rented car in a gas station not too far from where his family resided.

Over the last four months, they'd exchanged correspondence, phone calls, and eventually video calls with his mother. While it was true that he looked a lot like his father, he also saw some of his mother in him too. His dark complexion and cheekbones came from her.

She and his younger sister lived in a small, two-bedroom house with his mother's mother. His sister, Marcy, was their primary caregiver.

He learned that his mother, Ernestine, had tried to find him at various times over the years since he turned eighteen, but she never could. She'd had no idea that he changed his name and thought the fact that she couldn't find him was for the best because of the story behind his birth.

Layla covered his hand on the gearshift. "You ready?" she asked gently.

He'd insisted that she come because she'd been the catalyst for this reunion. She'd been the reason he finally sent a simple handwritten note on a card to his mother. That had finally culminated in this planned reunion.

"I'm ready."

He said the words, but the tightness in his stomach betrayed the severity of his fears. He didn't even know why he was nervous. They'd been in contact for months, yet he worried that rejection could still come. Perhaps when he walked up there and she saw him in the flesh, how much he looked like Chester, she'd change her mind about wanting a relationship with him.

Well, they'd driven over two hundred miles, so he might as well go that last mile to meet his family.

Rashad started the car and pulled out of the gas station and drove down the road past a row of small ranch houses on either side. Clammy palms gripping the wheel, he turned right into the subdivision. The GPS directed him to turn left down Acorn Street, and he followed those instructions. As soon as he did, he no longer needed the directions. He saw the house long before they pulled in front of it.

Outside the little brick ranch, there were red, blue, and yellow balloons tied to the mailbox. More balloons were tied to the railing on the little porch, and a huge welcome sign hung from the gutter that ran along the front.

Rashad eased the car in front of the house. Ernestine, Marcy, and his grandmother Kay were already waiting outside. He looked at Layla and tears burned his eyes when she smiled at him, biting her bottom lip. Without a word, he exited the car and walked toward the three people who were already coming down the driveway.

Ernestine was a tall, heavyset woman with her short Afro salted with gray. Marcy was shorter but thinner, her hair pulled into a thick ponytail. His grandmother Kay shuffled behind them wearing what looked to be her Sunday best, which included a string of pearls and her thin gray hair curled to frame her face.

Rashad stopped walking because his feet no longer could function. Rashad Greene, Mr. Confident, Mr. Suave, lost all his smooth and stood in the middle of the driveway, regressing into a little boy who simply wanted to be accepted. Wanted to be loved.

And he was.

Three sets of arms wrapped around him. He flung his arms around his mother's neck and held her tight as she cried. He brushed away a tear that fell onto his own cheek as he listened to her sobs. His sister rested her cheek against his bicep, and his grandmother took up the rear, whispering over and over again, "You're here. You're finally here."

When they released him, his mother gazed up into his face, each hand lightly touching his cheeks.

Looking deeply into his eyes, she said, "I never regretted having you. My only regret was not being brave enough to take you with me."

"It's okay. I don't blame you," Rashad whispered.

He wanted her to know this, though he'd said it before. He needed her to understand that he did not blame her for anything that had happened. The blame for the dissolution of their family and the pain she suffered lay squarely on the shoulders of the man sitting in a Texas prison.

"Layla's here." He signaled for Layla, who was standing several feet away, to come forward. She had talked to his family several times via video and on the phone. He slipped an arm around her and pulled her into his side. "As you know, she's the reason I had the courage to write to you. She's the best thing that ever happened to me," he said, gazing down at her.

"Welcome, to you too," his mother said, and then she treated Layla to a loving hug the same way she did him.

Mother. He had a hard time getting used to thinking in those terms.

They all went inside the small, quaint house. It was very clean and smelled like a bakery. The scent of fresh bread and cake perfumed the air and added to the homey atmosphere.

Rashad had brought a small photo album with pictures of him throughout the years. Over slices of pound cake and tall glasses of iced tea, they spent time going over the photos. He told them stories about his life and his accomplishments. His sister brought out photos as well, pictures of herself and their mother and grandmother over the years.

They spent the rest of the day there, which included eating a delicious dinner of roast, potatoes, and sauteed cabbage. While they talked over dinner and laughed and shared more stories, Rashad learned that his love for baking was a result of genetics. His grandmother used to run a bakery with his grandfather, but they had to close it when they fell on hard economic times. His mother learned to bake from her, and in fact for many years baked cakes and cookies and sold them out of her home as a way to make extra money.

Ernestine moved in with Kay after she and her second husband divorced, but she never lost her love of baking and was pleased to learn that Rashad had the same passion.

At almost ten o'clock, he reluctantly told his family they were going back to the hotel. He promised they'd be back tomorrow and wanted to take everyone to lunch, to which they readily agreed.

His grandmother had already gone to bed, so his sister and mother walked him and Layla to the door.

"We'll see you tomorrow," Ernestine said, voice quivering. He understood her emotional state and held onto her much longer than necessary before reluctantly pulling away.

As he and Layla walked down the driveway, he heard the door close behind them. He glanced down the street and up the street. The neighborhood was very quiet.

"Marcy does a lot of work," he remarked. "I think I'm going

to look into getting her some help, give her a break every now and again."

"That would be nice," Layla said. She took his hand. "I'm so happy for you, baby."

"Couldn't have done any of this without you.

"You would have gotten here eventually," Layla said.

"Maybe, but way in the distant future. I would have lost more time. Now I get to spend that time with them. Thank you. Really, for everything. For still being here."

"I love you, Rashad. I told you, I'm not going anywhere."

"I don't know what I did to deserve you, but I'm sure glad you're here."

He pulled her into his arms and kissed her forehead. "Let's go. Get some rest, and tomorrow when we come back, I'm getting that lemon pound cake recipe."

Layla laughed, tossing her head back. "I knew you were going to try to get that. It was so good. I'm sure you've already thought of a way to put your own twist on it."

"You already know."

They drove out of the neighborhood and toward the hotel. Tomorrow was a new day. The beginning of a new chapter in his life with the love of his life by his side.

Life was good.

ALSO BY DELANEY DIAMOND

Enjoy the other books in the Quicksand series about best friends
Tamika, Layla, and Dana!

Night and Day (Quicksand #4)

Anton doesn't know what to think of the sexy, baseball-bat-wielding
firebrand who disturbed his weekend rest. But somehow he gets sucked
into her charms, and after one night together, he can't get Tamika off
his mind.

What She Deserves (Quicksand #5)

Layla Fleming has changed since her breakup with Rashad Greene, and
a sex-only arrangement is all she'll consider now. But will that be
enough for *him*?

The Friend Zone (Quicksand #6)

Dana and Omar have a great friendship, but it's about to go through
some drastic changes.

A Powerful Attraction (Quicksand #1)

Alex and Sherry have a strong attraction that cannot be denied. But
when she learns the truth about him, will he end up losing her for good?

Audiobook samples and free short stories available at
www.delaneydiamond.com.

ABOUT THE AUTHOR

Delaney Diamond is the USA Today Bestselling Author of sweet, sensual, passionate romance novels. Originally from the U.S. Virgin Islands, she now lives in Atlanta, Georgia. She reads romance novels, mysteries, thrillers, and a fair amount of nonfiction. When she's not busy reading or writing, she's in the kitchen trying out new recipes, dining at one of her favorite restaurants, or traveling to an interesting locale.

Enjoy free reads and the first chapter of all her novels on her website. Join her mailing list to get sneak peeks, notices of sale prices, and find out about new releases.

Join her mailing list
www.delaneydiamond.com

facebook.com/DelaneyDiamond
twitter.com/DelaneyDiamond
bookbub.com/authors/delaney-diamond
pinterest.com/delaneydiamond

Made in the USA
Coppell, TX
20 June 2021

57759838R00089